WREATH OF FIRE

SMOKEY MOUNTAIN BEARS 2

TONI GRIFFIN

Edited by
ERIKA ORRICK

COPYRIGHT

About the Book You Have Purchased

This copy is intended for the original purchaser of this book ONLY. No part of this book may be reproduced, scanned, or distributed in any printed or electronic form without prior written permission from the authors. Please do not participate in or encourage piracy of copyrighted materials in violation of the author's rights. Purchase only authorized editions.

Cover Artist: Catherine Dair
Typographer: Freddy MacKay
Editor: Erika Orrick

First Edition

PUBLISHER
Mischief Corner Books, LLC

CONTENTS

DEDICATION

To Hank Edwards

Without your suggestion, we'd all be going nuts.
Much love, the Mischief Corner Crew.

And to Tim Brehme for egging Hank on.

Hats off, gentlemen.

TRADEMARKS ACKNOWLEDGEMENT

The author acknowledges the trademarked status and trademark owners of the following word marks mentioned in this work of fiction:

Chevy Silverado: General Motors, LLC
Ford: Ford Motor Company
Harley Davidson: Harley-Davidson, Inc.
iPad: Apple, Inc.

1

"*You*'re coming!"

Michael shook his head. "Christmas is a time for family. I'm not family."

"Rubbish." Patricia snorted.

Michael stared at her, not believing the noise that had come out of her mouth. The woman had been Alpha, for crying out loud. He somehow expected her to be a little more polished. Instead she was smiles, teasing, and warmth—all the things a mother should be. Something he had little experience with.

He tried to stick to his original argument. "I'm not, you can't deny that."

"Michael." Patricia sighed, sounding so exasperated as she brandished the egg-covered pastry brush in his direction, bits of liquid egg flinging everywhere. "You are a member of our sleuth. This automatically makes you family whether you share our bloodline or not. You should know this."

"But—"

The woman didn't give him a chance, just talked right over the top of him. "Plus, where do you think you're going to go? Huh? Christmas dinner is being held right here. You live here, for heaven's sake."

Michael grunted.

"You're celebrating Christmas with us and that's final. Or do I need to call Christian and get his ass over here to tell you?" The hard stare of his former Alpha and the no-nonsense tone was enough. He knew when he was beat.

"You win," he said.

Patricia smiled broadly at him, then went back to egg washing the pies for dinner. The pies smelled delicious and they hadn't even been cooked yet. His stomach rumbled. The one thing he hadn't had to worry about since moving in with his former Alpha was food. At the same time, he never knew what he was supposed to do, and ended up hovering a lot. He wanted to help. He *should* have helped.

"Would you be a dear and clean up that mess for me?" she asked with a knowing smile and pointed to the specks of spattered egg all over the counter.

"Sure." Michael grabbed a washcloth from the sink and wet it before ringing it out and heading over to clean up the mess. He looked around to make sure he'd gotten it all, and when satisfied, he rinsed out the cloth and hung it over the faucet. "Do you need a hand with anything else?"

"No, dear, I'm just about done."

Michael nodded and left her to it, walking away feeling a little less useless but still nursing the empty feeling inside him.

That had been three days ago.

His life was going nowhere fast. His father and older brother had betrayed the bear sleuth by drugging and attempting to kill Christian and had been banished from the area by their then-Alpha, Patricia. Michael hadn't heard from or seen his father or brother since, and he hoped it stayed that way.

He couldn't believe his luck when Christian, the Alpha's son and future Alpha himself, had told him he could stay if he wished. He'd hated his life up until that point, so he gladly took Christian up on his generous offer to remain in the sleuth. Michael had been genuinely happy when Christian had taken over as Alpha upon his thirtieth birthday a couple of months ago.

His father had treated both his sons like shit, but for some reason Jack loved their old man and followed him religiously. The only reason Michael had ever followed the man was to avoid a beating, and even then, only when he was still healing from the latest assault. Being a shifter, it said a lot about the abuse he'd taken that he would still be recovering from those beatdowns days after.

His father had been an abusive drunk. A hard thing to do with their metabolisms as shifters. The days his temper flared while intoxicated were some of the worst in Michael's memories. He'd always try to shift and hide on those days. Sometimes he didn't manage to, and those days were the hardest. Michael trembled as the echoes of those moments haunted his heart. He was convinced his father's heavy drinking had affected the shifter inside him and lowered his tolerance to substances they were usually immune to. Michael couldn't remember the last time his father had shifted. He wouldn't be surprised if the bear inside his dad had died from abuse and neglect.

Michael couldn't even imagine what that would be like. It would be like losing half of himself. He shuddered at the idea of losing that baser, more primal side of himself. His bear was a piece of him as much as he was a piece of his bear. They were two halves of one whole. He never felt freer than when his could shift into his second form and run with the other members of their sleuth.

Even still, his dad had been a large man and had a lot of power behind him. It was hard to stand up to someone who had taken up so much presence in his life, especially since the abuse had escalated over the years. Michael had never been a strong shifter, and he'd become so accustomed to cowering in front of his father that the thought of fighting back hadn't occurred to him when he was younger. He had gotten stuck in a victim's mindset and hadn't been able to change.

Living with his former Alpha, having the support from her and the family resources had helped him see the abuse and understand it better—and himself.

It'll take time. Something Michael didn't feel he had. He wasn't some child that needed rescuing.

For the first time since he could remember, people cared about him and what he needed. He didn't know what to do with that. He hadn't done anything to deserve the way Patricia and everyone looked after him.

Sometimes their happy family life made it hard to understand the feelings Michael felt stirring inside him.

Being a mere week away from celebrating his first Christmas without his family—not that there had been much celebrating when he had lived at home with his dad and brother—and Michael couldn't find any remorse about it. Any money his father brought into the house he spent on alcohol, and he only occasionally had remembered to buy a few groceries.

Michael hadn't remembered what it was like to have a full stomach until he'd come to live with Patricia and her mate, George. Having a full stomach was a blessing, but it also made it hard not to want to check and make sure there was enough food for everyone. He needed to *know* they had enough food. Then there was how everyone talked around him. Oftentimes, it made him feel more than a little lost. He had missed so much school growing up, both with his bruises and running the errands his father had sent him on—the man not caring that Michael was supposed to be getting an education—that he hadn't managed to come close to graduating.

Not like Patricia and her family. They were all successful and had work.

He barely had an education, and he didn't have a job, which meant no money. The clothes they had managed to recover from his father's house before the man had burned everything were thin and threadbare. The Packards had been generous and purchased him some new clothes, especially when winter had hit, but Michael hated being dependent on others. They had already been generous enough and he felt horrible about being an extra burden on them. He wanted to be his own man, earning his own money for once in his life. He had tried to help as much as he could around the house with whatever George and Patricia might need, but there were only so many things that needed to be done.

What Michael really wanted was to go back to school and get his GED. Yes, he was twenty-two, but he didn't care. Michael didn't want to waste his entire life wondering *what if*. He'd spoken to Patricia about it at length and was grateful that she was supportive of the idea. She had offered to help in any way she could. Patricia even offered to coach him through the paperwork to start classes.

That help, of course, became one more thing to add to the ever-growing list of what Michael owed the Packards.

But first Michael had to get through Christmas.

He still wasn't entirely comfortable with the idea of spending Christmas with the Packards. He truly believed the time was supposed to be for families. It was not his time or space to intrude on, and her insisting on him being here only made it more obvious about what he never had. He no longer had a family, had barely had one even when his father and brother were around.

He had no one to call his own, no one to look out for, and no one to love him.

Michael sighed as he lay on the bed in the room he had been given and stared at the ceiling. He felt so alone it wasn't funny. The Packards were lovely people, and he appreciated everything they'd done, but he wanted someone for himself. One person to love.

It had to be easier starting with something smaller than having one's former alpha try to fix everything for him.

Is that what mothers do? Fix everything?

Michael thought about his new Alpha, Christian, and how he was with his mate, Vincent. The pair were still newly bonded, only being together for roughly four months. It made for interesting territorial displays on his Alpha's part—or that might have to do with his mate being human. Though Vincent seemed to adapt quicker than Michael had expected. Mere weeks after he'd met Christian, the human had packed up his life in Las Vegas and moved to the mountains here in Tennessee. What would it be like to have that kind of devotion from someone? Michael doubted he'd ever find out. If his own father couldn't give a shit about him, what hope did he have that someone else would?

How would someone like him, who was still trying to get a handle on basic life skills, ever find a partner interested in someone who couldn't even graduate high school?

He looked at his watch and groaned. It was only early afternoon. The days tended to move so slowly now that he had nothing to do and nowhere to go. Not that he'd really had much to do before. Daytime television sucked, so he tended to stay well away from it. Running in his bear half could only take up so much of his day.

Michael had done barely anything that day, but he was tired.

Maybe it was best to take a nap? But he didn't want to sleep the entire afternoon away, since he wanted to do something nice for Patricia and George before they got home. Like make dinner. He could do that much. He wasn't the best of cooks, but it was the thought that counted. Hopefully the Packards agreed.

Michael rolled over on his bed and got comfortable. The crisp, clean sheets and the wonderful aroma that went along with them surrounded Michael and he sighed in happiness. He couldn't believe the difference some days. Nothing ever felt clean at his father's house, no matter how many times he washed them.

He pulled the spare pillow close and held it to him as he closed his eyes. Michael wondered briefly what it would be like to share his bed with someone else. Preferably a tall, handsome, muscled someone, but that would only ever be a dream.

MICHAEL STOOD THERE AND STARED FOR MOMENT, completely paralyzed with shock and fear as the flames licked up the wall. Within moments, the fire had spread to the evergreen wreath Patricia had hung the previous week. Once that went up, the pops and sparks from the pine sap had reached the curtains just off to the side, and they too had caught alight. The smoke was dark, thick, and cloying.

What had he done?

One minute he was cooking dinner as best he

could, but then he heard his phone ringing so he raced to the bedroom to answer it. He didn't get many calls. Michael had assumed it would be important. It wasn't, just a damn telemarketer.

When he walked back into the kitchen, he found it going up in flames.

"Oh shit, oh shit, oh shit," Michael whispered as he quickly dialed 911.

He rushed forward and reached for the water tap. Just as the operator picked up, the smoke alarms started going crazy.

Michael burst in to tears.

All he had wanted to do was make dinner for the Packards.

"911, what's your emergency?"

"I just set the kitchen on fire." Michael sobbed as he tried to gather water and splash it on the fire. That didn't seem to be doing much, though. Then he noticed the gas stovetop was still on and he quickly moved to turn it off, the heat incredible the closer he got.

"Sir? Sir?"

"The kitchen! It's on fire," he said again, panic crawling across his skin, making it tight.

"Have you moved to a safe location, sir?"

"It's on fire!" Why didn't the operator understand? No matter how nice the Packards were, no way would they keep him in the house if he screwed up like this. What was he going to do? What would they do when they came home?

"Sir! We need your address. Have you exited the house?"

"What no? I need to..." Michael hiccupped. "Need to make it stop."

"Your address, sir."

"Right." Michael gave the operator the address and his details then hung up. Their talking only distracted him more and he *needed* to stop the fire. The flames kept getting bigger and he couldn't just stand there and do nothing.

Alpha was going to be so upset with him.

Michael grabbed a tea towel and started batting at the flames. They were everywhere and the smoke filled the room. He wiped the tears from his eyes with the back of his hand, the towel not doing anything to combat the flames. Of course it wouldn't. It was a damn towel. How stupid could he be?

Then again, he was pretty dumb. A dropout like him would be.

How could he make it stop? Michael coughed hard, smoke filling his lungs. His eyes watered from the harsh sting in the air.

The fire extinguisher! Patricia had shown him one when they took him in. *Idiot.*

There was a fire extinguisher in the pantry. He raced the three steps it took to get there and yanked open the door.

He blinked several times trying to clear his vision from the tears and smoke before he could finally focus and find the shiny red extinguisher.

Lifesaver.

They won't kill me. I'm not dead. The whole house won't burn down.

Michael quickly grabbed it and turned back to the

flames spreading from the stove. He pulled the pin and pointed the hose toward the fire, then depressed the top handle. The chemical spray managed to smother the flames on the stove but ran out of juice shortly after that.

It was only a small household extinguisher, and Michael hadn't expected much, still, his heart stuttered. He'd hoped it would have lasted for a little longer than it did. The heat from the flames was intense, and Michael started coughing as the smoke and heat affected him. His eyes burned while he stood rooted to the spot, unable to move, staring as the room went up in flames.

How the hell was he going to explain this to Patricia and George?

2

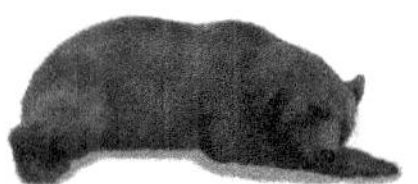

am grunted as he lifted the heavy weight above his chest. The two hundred and thirty pounds he had on the bar was a piece of cake for him, but if he started loading the bar with upward of four to five hundred pounds, his human coworkers might start to get a little suspicious. Even though the weight was light for him, in relative terms, he still got a workout, which was what he wanted.

Keeping in shape was something he and his fellow firefighters worked on. Made the job easier.

The grunting helped keep any speculation about his more animalistic side at bay. It was what his coworkers did when they did reps. Blending in with humans was a thing shifters had to do.

"Come on, Cam, two more," Evan said from above him, his hands at the ready to catch the bar if Cam failed to lift the weight.

He wouldn't, but he put on a good show nonetheless.

Sweat beaded on his forehead, more a result of the overheated room with half a dozen men working out than from any real strain on his part. Cam controlled the weight back down to his chest before lifting once again. His reps complete, Evan helped him steady the bar and place it back in the supports.

Cam took a deep breath and sat up on the black leather, padded bench, pulling the towel from under him. He wiped his face and arms, sighing.

Downtime had its perks, but waiting around on shift also had its pitfalls.

Evan patted him on the shoulder. "Nice set, man. Any time you need a spot, just holler."

"Will do. Thanks."

Cam nodded in his direction and surreptitiously watched as Evan walked away, his ass encased nicely in his workout clothes. He quickly glanced away before anyone could catch him looking. He hadn't exactly moved to the most gay-friendly state in the country.

Not that home had been. Tennessee was its own beast, though.

He hadn't been in Gatlinburg long enough to feel out the rest of the guys in his unit and get their opinions on the matter. For now, he planned to keep his head down, do his job, and prove to the others that he knew what he was doing. Hopefully by the time they did find out about his sexuality, they wouldn't care.

Cam could never picture himself doing anything else.

All he had ever wanted to do after his family home

had gone up in flames when he was just a boy was become a firefighter. His mom and dad had gotten Cam, his brother, and two sisters out of the house safely, but they had lost everything.

Not being able to stop the fire or help in any way had left a huge impact on his adolescent mind.

Cam still remembered standing on the street in front of his house as it burned to the ground before his eyes. All the neighbors had come out and gathered around them to watch as well. An electrical fault had been the cause for the disaster. At the time, Cam had been devastated at the loss of all his belongings. Now, though, he was just thankful his entire family had survived. Cam had attended far too many fires where people had died not to know how lucky he was.

With another grunt, he eyed the exercise room to see what had opened up. His muscles felt nice and loose after his workout. He wiped down the bench and hopped up.

Wanting a cooldown, Cam jumped on one of the empty treadmills. He cranked the speed up to seven miles and set an incline of three. After twenty minutes, the sweat was pouring off him again, and Cam reduced the speed until he pressed the Stop button. He grabbed his towel and gave himself a quick wipe down before he cleaned his machine and headed for the showers.

The day had been a slow one. Only two call-outs so far and one of them had been for a false alarm. Cam hoped the rest of his shift would be just as slow. The waiting around got to everyone, but his was the type of work where not getting called-out meant no fires. No fires were a good thing. He stepped into the showers to wash all the sweat off—the warm water working wonders on his muscles. Even with the heaters on in the station due to the cold temperatures outside, standing under the spray of a hot shower was something Cam enjoyed immensely.

Being originally from Montana, Cam wasn't a stranger to snow on the ground, and thanks to his bear half, the cold didn't affect him anywhere near as bad as it did humans.

Moving halfway across the country had been a hard choice to make for Cam. He'd never lived anywhere other than Montana. His entire family was still there, but Cam had decided it was time to branch out. He wanted a family of his own, and he wasn't finding it in Montana. Gay and Montana hadn't been an easy thing either. He doubted he would find someone in Gatlinburg either, but at least he was trying somewhere different.

Cam figured if he wanted to find his mate, if there even was one out there for him, that he needed to get off his ass and look instead of waiting and expecting his mate to come to him.

Being a brown grizzly bear caused a few problems, though. He didn't stand out too badly if anyone happened to spot him back home. Tennessee, however, had only black bears, and if anyone were to spot Cam here, he would more than likely stick out like a sore thumb and cause one hell of a panic.

He'd only been in town for two weeks and hadn't had an opportunity to shift and go for a run through the beautiful forests yet. He had an appointment with the local sleuth Alpha in two days, when he was next off shift, to get permission to use the land or even join the sleuth if he was able.

Cam didn't know what his chances were of that happening. Hopefully the Alpha wasn't a jerk. He didn't know a great deal about the local Alpha, only that he was brand new to the job and that he'd taken over from his mother.

"You goin' to spend all day in there, Cam?" Evan asked, snapping his towel. "Avoiding chores?"

"Maybe. I actually broke a sweat did you?"

"Ha!"

Pierce chuckled as he walked by. "Cam's got you there, man."

"I worked out!" Evan protested.

"You mean standing over me as I did reps? Sure ya did."

"What! I didn't just spot you."

Mark snorted. "You're right, you helped spot me too."

"It was my leg day," Evan insisted. "We have less machines geared toward that."

"Sure," Cam agreed, chuckling. "We all know you have to work what assets you have."

The guys erupted in laughter, louder than before. Everyone piled right on, teasing and razzing on each other as they washed away the grime.

"Y'all can fuck off," Evan grumbled.

Cam finished up in the shower and dried himself, leaving Evan to the others. Teach him to mess with Cam. He got dressed in his uniform, blue pants and a long-sleeved black shirt with the department logo over the left breast then pulled on heavy socks and shoved his feet in his boots before he bent and laced them up tight.

The others filtered in and got dressed, too, chatting away before leaving to give the trucks a washdown.

He followed behind, making his way through the building and into the truck bay where other guys were working on washing the engines. The glass bay doors were down, keeping as much heat as possible inside. The late afternoon sun was slowly sinking on the horizon.

Cam was just about to pick up a polishing rag and join his workmates when the alarm went off.

He rushed the few feet over to his locker and suited up, stepping into his pants, then pulling on his jacket and grabbed up his helmet and breathing gear.

Evan was right there next to him, suiting up, along with Mark and Pierce. Cam jumped up into a truck as the bay door lifted for them. He rode in the back, still not knowing the area well enough to drive. Pierce had that honor today and as they pulled from the station, the lights and sirens flicked on.

Cars gave way to them most of the time, Pierce swearing like a sailor on the few occasions motorists refused to move. "Fucking idiots, do they not see the giant red truck barreling up their asses?"

Cam just shook his head. No matter where you were in the world, you would always come across that one person that didn't move. Admittedly, there were times on narrow roads and such where it was difficult to find somewhere to pull over and let them pass.

Soon enough, they were pulling up outside a lovely house at the edge of the suburbs backed by forest. Lovely except for the smoke. That put a damper on things. As much as Cam could appreciate a house like that for his bear, the idea of a fire starting here and spreading was horrific. When the call came in, they had been informed it was a kitchen fire.

They could see small amounts of smoke, but nothing major. *Yet.*

"Doesn't look like things are out of control yet," Mark said as they opened the door and jumped down from the high cab.

Pierce nodded. "Operator said the caller hung up on them. Sounded panic. Keep that in mind as we go in. I don't see anyone outside."

"Sure thing," they answered.

Evan swore and Cam understood completely. Panicking people in a fire meant bad news. It got people killed.

He secured his helmet and checked his breathing gear that was strapped to his back, then quickly made his way to the back of the truck with the others. They opened the roller doors, and Evan and Mark started removing the crosslay hose. Cam quickly connected it to the line, and Pierce got in place to control the panel. Suited up and ready to go, Cam got into place between Evan and Mark as they grabbed the hose and crossed the small front yard to enter the house.

"Fire department," Evan called out as they entered the premises.

Someone coughed from the direction the smoke was coming from. Not what they wanted to hear.

Cam didn't pay attention to his surroundings as they made their way through to the kitchen, the scent of smoke and fire thick and heavy now.

He took it all in in a heartbeat: the man standing off to the side, coughing, holding his shirt over his mouth, the fire eating its way up the walls and over the countertop, the foam covering the top of the stove, and the empty fire extinguisher lying on the ground where it had been dropped.

In front of him, Evan radioed out to Pierce that they were in position. Mark detached from behind them to take care of the occupant of the house and search for any others that might still be inside. The rush of water came quickly, the hose going from flat and light one moment to stiff and heavy the next.

Evan and Cam attacked the fire, drowning it in water to stop its spread into the rest of the house. They heard Mark give the all clear for the property not long after the last of the flames finally died out. The fire hadn't been large and all consuming by any stretch, but it was still big enough to cause a great deal of damage in the kitchen.

They soaked the walls through, and the cabinets. Chances were there was no saving those. The appliances were totaled, too—the stove was destroyed. The metal had warped from the heat of the flames.

Water pooled on the floor. They doused the area liberally, wanting to make sure any hot spots didn't have a chance to reignite.

Someone would need a new kitchen.

The fire probably hadn't had enough time to cause

any structural problems, but the fire inspector would be the one to make that call. Still, the family was lucky the flames hadn't spread farther. A kitchen was replaceable. When Evan eventually gave the all clear inside, Pierce shut off the water, and the hose went slack in their hands once again.

Cam surveyed the kitchen again, his heart aching. It was so close to Christmas. This was going to hurt. Besides, it never hurt to double-or-triple check things to make sure the fire was well and truly out.

The blackened wall and scorched ceiling would need replacing and painting. No doubt there. The remnants of what used to be curtain and the shell of a wreath hung in tatters from the wall. The melted countertops and the charcoaled remains of what Cam assumed was supposed to be dinner, sat on the ruined stovetop.

Everything was saturated, which he'd always believed to be preferable to an entire house being lost to fire.

Cam took a couple of steps to the side of the kitchen, then leaned over the charred counter and opened the window. The temperature inside dropped immediately, but the remnants of smoke needed to dissipate and this would help. It would also help with getting rid of some of the smell, although the house would more than likely need a thorough cleaning to rid it completely of the scent left by the fire.

He removed his helmet and breathing gear and tucked it under his arm, then turned back to Evan, waiting for what he wanted to do next. He was higher on the food chain than Cam was. That meant he ended up with most of the grunt work.

"Would you mind taking that back out while I have a look at things in here?" Evan asked, already stepping over toward the counter.

"Sure, man."

"Thanks."

Cam picked up the hose and threw it over his shoulder so the heavy nozzle dangled down his front. He held it in place with one hand as he made his way back through the house, thankful the damage had been contained to the kitchen area.

His nose twitched with every step he took closer to the front door. He smelled the acrid scent of fire, but underneath, there was something else he couldn't quite put his finger on. Something not burned kitchen. Whatever it was smelled divine, calling to Cam on a primal level that he couldn't make sense of.

Now wasn't the time to get distracted. They had people to help.

As he stepped outside, a mop of honey-brown hair caught his attention. Cam turned to look at the young man. He was probably the one Mark escorted out and Cam wanted to make sure he was okay. His breath caught.

Something inside Cam's chest squeezed tight just from setting his eyes on the young man.

It wasn't the guy's state of confusion, either.

Something...

The honey-brown hair stuck up in all sorts of disarrayed angles, as if the man had run his fingers through it a million times. Cam bet he had. His face was blotchy and his dark brown eyes were red and puffy from crying. Black patches covered his chest and face. Cam could still see tear tracks down the man's cheeks. He obviously wasn't a graceful crier. The thought had Cam smiling.

Unsettling thought. He rubbed his chest. It made no sense. Why would he smile when this man had just lost part of his house?

The young man wasn't overly large, in either height or body mass, but he wasn't tiny either. Cam thought he looked to be *just* right. The breeze blew and with it was that amazing scent that he had smelled inside. Cam breathed deeply for a moment, then paused as his entire body went on alert. His bear roared to life, growling and clawing to be let loose to track that delicious scent.

Cam forced his animal down, confused and worried about his lack of control. There was no way he could shift in front of Mark and Pierce, who were human, let alone the young man. He took another deep breath.

It felt like a damn bell was clanging inside him, his muscles tense and his cock painful as blood rushed south and he figured out he was tucked in the worst possible position.

"What in living..." Cam muttered, still staring.

It was at that point he realized two things.

One, the young man standing with Mark wasn't human.

Two, with the way his body had just flown into must-fuck-now mode, Cam knew, without a shadow of a doubt, that he'd just met his mate.

ichael could feel eyes on him. He knew the firefighter was probably staring at him, thinking he was a complete and utter idiot for not being able to cook a simple meal like fried chicken without setting the kitchen on fire. Or maybe the guy thought he was stupid for trying to put it out himself. Or not leaving the house like a sane person would.

The laundry list for stupidity was rather long at the moment.

Well, the man would be right. He was an idiot. Michael ducked his head, not wanting to see the condemnation he knew would be in those eyes.

He still had no idea how he was going to explain all this to Patricia and George. Michael contemplated writing them a quick note—to apologize and to let them know he would send them money to pay for the damages when he got a job—before packing his bag and leaving. Hopefully he would be able to get away before either of them got home.

There was no way he could face their condemnation and wrath for what he'd done. His flight response was in full gear, and more than anything, he wished he could shift and run.

He had plenty of hiding spots his father hadn't found yet. The Packards probably couldn't find them either.

A loud squeal of tires stopped his conversation with—what was his name?

The vehicle came to an abrupt halt followed by the frantic call of, "Michael! Michael!"

He sighed, knowing it was already too late. He winced and curled in on himself. Better to make a smaller target than a bigger one. He glanced up as Patricia raced across the lawn, barreling full steam ahead. She didn't run to the house to see the damage like Michael thought she would. Nor did she raise her fists. Instead she ran right up to him, engulfed him in a hug, and held him close.

"Jesus, I was so worried. I saw the smoke and then the fire engine," she said as she held him tighter for a few seconds before letting him go. She looked him up and down. Her brows were up and forehead creased. "You're okay? You're not hurt, are you?"

Michael shook his head, tears falling as he tried and failed to talk past the lump that had lodged in his throat. Finally he whispered, "I'm so sorry."

"Now, now. We'll have none of that, boy," Patricia said soothingly as she reached up and wiped away his tears. "It was an accident. Well, I'm assuming it was. You didn't set out to burn down my house, did you?"

"No, ma'am," Michael said on a sob. He couldn't seem to stop.

"That's what I thought. Now stop your crying. You weren't hurt, and we have insurance to cover this type of thing. Plus, you've given me the perfect excuse to finally get my kitchen remodel that George has been putting off for the last ten years." Patricia smiled at him, then pulled him into another hug. "I'm so glad you're okay. That's what's important."

Mother's do fix things.

Michael held on for dear life. He had no idea what he'd done to garner such understanding and acceptance from her, but he wouldn't look a gift horse in the mouth. All he'd wanted was to do something nice to show his appreciation to this wonderful family, and he'd managed to fuck that up royally.

Except she hadn't reacted the way she should've. Nothing like his father would've. Patricia had been concerned about him first. She hadn't been angry with him. She had held him like he was what mattered.

Michael pulled away when his body started reacting funny and he felt uncomfortable. Why the hell was he suddenly sprouting wood while hugging a woman he thought of as a surrogate mother? Heat bloomed in his cheeks as he burned in embarrassment. His flushed cheeks would just add to the complete mess that he was sure he looked.

"Come on," Patricia said, leading him over to the

side of the drive. "Let's get out of the way while these nice firemen finish up."

Michael had completely forgotten all about the firefighters. He remembered one of them coming over and leading him outside while others battled the blaze, but Michael had been too distraught to pay too much attention to them. He thought the man's name might have been Martin or something similar, but he couldn't remember. Michael looked away from Patricia at the men on the lawn stretching out a hose and packing it away. His gaze was caught immediately in the intense blue eyes of one of the firefighters he had yet to meet.

What?

His heartbeat increased and his head became fuzzy, making it impossible to look away from the man—who stood no more than a half a dozen feet in front of him. The man wasn't what most people would have considered gorgeous. Yes, he was tall, probably close to half a foot taller than Michael. He obviously had muscles. Doing the job he did Michael doubted there was an ounce of fat on the man anywhere, and the bulky bright yellow protective outfit made him look even larger than he was.

His dark brown hair was cut short, shaved close on the sides with only the barest hint of length on the top. His nose was large, his eyebrows thick and bushy, but the blue of his eyes shone through. The man's lips were surrounded by a beard that followed the contours of his face. This man was obviously well groomed, the beard was trimmed close and neatly, and Michael wanted to feel it against his naked skin.

What? That…that was insane. Why would that man even look at someone like him?

His body was going haywire and Michael didn't know why. It wasn't until he took a deep breath that it finally clicked. The man in front of him wasn't human, he was a shifter, and he smelled very much like *mate*.

"Michael? Is everything all right?" Patricia asked him. "You're sounding scared. What's happened?"

He hadn't even realized he'd made the small whimpering noise until she asked.

Michael shook his head. This could not be happening. No way could he meet his mate now, when he'd just proven to everyone what a complete and total fuckup he was. He couldn't deal with this right now. Not even a little bit. His mate had seen how much of a loser he was, and they hadn't even gotten to the high school dropout part. He turned to Patricia.

"I'm sorry," he whispered again.

Michael would be saying that for the rest of his life.

He turned and darted for the house, people calling after him. Michael wasn't thinking. He just knew he had to get away from everything and the only way he knew how was to shift. He raced through the house, the scent of the fire strong and cloying as soon as he stepped through the front door. He made it to the back door, pushing it open with a bang. He ran outside and across the back lawn.

Michael ignored the calls from Patricia and a deep sexy voice he could only assume was the man he thought might be his mate. Their heavy steps thudded behind him, but he wasn't stopping. He vaulted over the back fence, not bothering to waste time on the locked gate, and ran into the forest.

He ran barefoot through the trees, thankful for his shifter side. The temperature had to be close to freezing. A bitter wind blew through the forest, causing Michael to shiver despite his higher than average body temperature.

When he was certain he was out of sight, Michael stopped and took a moment. His heart pounded furiously in his chest. Why did the world have to be so cruel? Things were finally starting to look up: he was going to go back to school and get his GED, and then he could decide what he wanted to do with his life. Instead, he nearly burned down the house of the only people who had ever been kind to him, proving to the one person he'd wanted since forever that he was a complete loser.

Michael stripped quickly. It was too cold to stay still for too long. He thought about his bear, concentrated, and felt the shift start to take over. Within moments, he was standing on all fours, the thick black coat of his fur keeping him warm from the icy winds. Michael lifted his head and roared out all his frustration, then took off into the woods.

Since life wanted to laugh at him, it was best if he was left alone.

CAM STOOD AND WATCHED, TOO STUNNED TO REACT AT first, as his mate took off into the house. As soon as the older woman ran past him, Cam was following along behind.

"What are you doing, Marsh?" The yell from Pierce slowed him for a second only.

"I'll be back in a minute," he answered.

The woman was calling for his mate and thought he would give it a try as well. He didn't expect it to make a difference.

"Michael," he called out. His mate stumbled a little, maybe he'd heard Cam's voice as they made it through the back door, but the man kept on running, over the back fence and into the forest.

What in...well, that is one way to meet your mate.

As much as Cam would have loved to chase the younger man down and simply hold him until he calmed, he couldn't do that. He was on the clock and had to work. He would be back, though.

Cam turned to look at the distraught woman. He wondered if this was his mate's mother. They didn't smell the same, but Michael could have been adopted. The woman was powerful, Cam could tell that.

"What in the world was all that about?" The woman turned and looked at him, her steely gaze pinning him in place. If Cam were a weaker man, he would have been squirming where he stood.

The foot shuffle he did was *not* a twitch. Not a big one. He looked behind him to the back door to the house, thankful it must have closed behind him.

"Ma'am, I believe that was my mate who just took off into the trees."

The woman cocked one eyebrow and folded her arms across her chest. "And just who the hell are you, young man, and why don't I know about you being in my territory?"

Her territory? Cam was confused but started talking fast. "I'm sorry, I was under the impression a Mr. Christian Packard was the Alpha here. I might have my information wrong. If so, I'm sorry about that. Name's Cameron Marsh. Grizzly. Just moved here from Montana. I have an appointment with Mr. Packard when I finish my shift the day after tomorrow."

The woman sighed and her rigid stance seemed to deflate a little.

"Christian is my son. Sorry, recent transfer. I'm used to being the one in charge." She shrugged.

Cam chuckled lightly. "Understandable, ma'am."

"Oh, for heaven's sake, stop calling me *ma'am*. My name is Patricia Packard."

"Yes, ma'am," Cam said automatically.

She just stared at him. Hard.

Cam grinned. "Sorry."

She sighed. "So, you believe Michael's your mate?"

"I believe so, yes." Just as Cam finished his sentence, the back door opened and Evan poked his head out.

"Everything okay out here?" he asked.

"Yep."

"Time to go, Cam. Got to get back to the station before the chief starts wondering where the hell we are," Evan said. As his unit member squinted at him, Cam thought he might have been trying to determine if Cam was telling the truth or not. "The fire inspector should be calling to schedule a time to come out and inspect the damage shortly, Mrs. Packard."

"Thank you, Evan," she answered.

Cam nodded. "I'll be with you in a minute."

"I'll wait out the front with the others. Don't be too long." Evan closed the door behind himself.

Cam looked longingly toward the forest beyond. What he really wanted was to chase after his wayward mate. His bear didn't like the fact that he wasn't going after him.

"Come back when you can. Hopefully Michael will be in a better frame of mind by then," Patricia said to him soothingly. She could obviously tell how conflicted he was.

"I'll be back the moment I get off shift, but as I said before, that won't be for two more days. Can you please let Michael know that I'm working and that's the only reason why I haven't come back for him?" Cam wanted his mate to know that if it wasn't for his job, he would be there.

"I'll make sure and let him know. You should probably get going," Patricia said.

Cam sighed and took one last long look at the woods before he turned and walked back into the house. The kitchen was still a mess. His helmet clutched in his hand, Cam made his way through the house and out the front door to the truck that sat idling, waiting for him.

He climbed up into the cab and threw his helmet on the bench seat next to him. Pierce stepped on the gas and drove them away from the place where Cam's life had changed in an instant.

His mate. He couldn't believe he'd been lucky enough actually to meet the man, and less than a week before Christmas. That was like the best Christmas present ever. Now all he needed to do was convince the man they belonged together. Cam had no idea what Michael's story was, hell, he didn't even know the man's last name. He assumed it was Packard, but he didn't know that. Patricia hadn't said one way or the other.

Of course, their Christmas just had a major wrench tossed into it. Poor Michael looked devastated about the house.

It wasn't the whole house, though. Just the kitchen.

Still, something like a house fire shook up a lot of people. Cam understood that.

Michael was younger than he had expected his mate to be. Cam had just turned thirty-one. Michael looked to be in his early twenties. Cam didn't care, though. His mate could have blue skin, and he would still grow to love the man. Cam might think the skin a little freaky to start, but he wouldn't hold it against him. The only thing that was a deal breaker for Cam was someone who wasn't male. Cam had tried that in his youth. Well, it would be more accurate to say that he had tried to try. He didn't get very far.

Broke Lou Ann's heart in the process. That had been his hardest break-up to date. He had never meant to hurt her. Growing up where they had, fitting in was what everyone tried to do, except he couldn't.

Definitely gay.

By the look and smell of his mate—what he could smell over the scent of the fire—his mate was definitely male.

"Everything cool, Cam?" Mark asked from up front.

"Yeah, man. Just met someone I wasn't expecting."

"Care to elaborate?" Pierce asked, looking over his shoulder at Cam quickly before returning his eyes to the road in front of him.

"Not just yet." He smiled wanly, hating the fact that he was stuck at work for so long before he would even get the chance to speak to his mate.

Cam resigned himself to the longest two days of his life.

His bear was already on the outs with him, not happy in the slightest that they'd left their mate behind. His skin felt tight and his body still thrummed with the remembered scent of his mate. His cock had yet to go down and was still at an awkward angle, Cam having forgotten about his discomfort in the face of his mate running out on him.

He couldn't exactly fix his problem in here, as it would take more than the quick adjustment. It would have to wait until he was back at the station and he had a little privacy. What Cam needed was a helping hand to make it feel better.

Too bad his mate wasn't there to help fix it. Then again, if he was skittish, it was probably for the best.

When they returned, all the not so glamorous parts of being a firefighter started. The hose they used was pulled out and checked before being packed away properly again. All the equipment, including their breathing gear, was checked, refilled, and stowed away for the next call. The truck was cleaned and all the paperwork completed.

Several hours later, Cam finally found himself with a couple of minutes to spare. Even in all that time, his prick had barely gone down. He'd had no idea meeting his mate would cause such a reaction in his body. He practically raced to the bathroom. The second he was behind the closed door of a stall, he unzipped his fly and stuck his hand inside his briefs to fish out his aching prick.

Cam couldn't believe how much relief he felt simply by moving his cock. He sighed as he leaned against the stall wall and closed his eyes, imagining his mate who had stood in front of him that evening. Even with the red puffy eyes and the tear streaks down his checks, Michael was gorgeous. He was a lucky bear to get someone as sweet looking as his mate. Cam applied a little pressure to his dick and slowly stroked his hand from the base to the tip.

He clenched his jaw to stop the moan that nearly escaped. The last thing he wanted to do was announce to the entire station that he was jacking off in the john. Thankfully, he was so keyed up that this wouldn't take long at all. He moved his hand in smooth strokes over his hard flesh, just the way he liked it, applying pressure at just the right time. Cam pictured his wayward mate.

His mate's skin looked silky smooth under all that ash. Cam wanted to run his tongue up the side of Michael's neck and taste him. He could picture how much his mate would enjoy being loved on, taken care of. Any tears would be from pleasure, not because some fire upset him. More than anything, he wanted a taste of Michael. His mouth tingled, wanting to savor the flavor of his mate. To have Michael's mouth on him. Cam's fingers itched to run through the light brown, almost golden strands of Michael's hair, causing his bear to pace restlessly inside him.

His dick throbbed and ached in his tight grip. He increased the speed of his hand, thrusting his cock in and out of his fist. Cam licked the tips of his thumb and finger on his free hand, then reached down and played with his slit. He bit down hard on his lip, tasting the copper tang of blood. When his hips thrust one last time, Cam came in a torrent of hot semen. His body went boneless. If not for the stall wall he was already leaning against, Cam would have ended up on the floor.

He took a few deep breaths, in through his nose and out through his mouth, in an effort to regulate his breathing and bring his pulse back to normal. His right hand still held his softening member, coated in cum. But it wasn't just in his hand. Cam reluctantly pushed off the wall and bent down to retrieve some toilet paper to clean himself up. He'd made a mess, and Cam was forced to clean that up as well. He couldn't just walk away and leave his spunk splattered on the toilet and floor.

His bear still wasn't happy, even after the orgasm. Cam tried to soothe his animal, knowing the second he got off shift, no matter how exhausted he was, he would be seeking out his mate.

He couldn't wait to actually get some time and talk with the young man. Cam wanted to know everything about him but he wasn't going to rush things. After all, they had their entire lives to learn everything they needed to about each other.

Happy he was clean enough, Cam gave his clothes one more inspection. The last thing he wanted to do was walk out, join the rest of the crew, and announce what he had just been doing. He wasn't the only guy to ever wring one out at work and he hadn't taken that long from start to finish, being as keyed up as he had been. But he still didn't want everyone to know what he'd been up to.

Cam didn't give anything away as he walked out of the bathroom and headed for the communal area. No one said anything to him, and Cam walked over to one of the large couches and took a seat next to Paula, one of their paramedics.

"Anything decent on?" he asked as he got comfortable, his body now sated and relaxed.

"Not a damn thing, man," Paula replied as she surfed through the channels, only stopping long enough to see what was on and decide she didn't want to watch it before moving on to the next.

Night had fallen after they had returned to the station. The light from inside reflected off the darkened windows. Cam watched as a couple of the guys sat at one of the large dining tables and played a game of cards. At the other end, Mark sat typing away on his laptop. In the living area, two more guys had joined Cam and Paula on the couches. Pierce pulled out a book to read instead of watching Paula flick through channels.

Over in the kitchen Martin, one of the old timers, stirred a large pot of what Cam's nose was telling him was chili. He groaned as he inhaled the delectable aroma. Cam hadn't been here very long, but everyone on shift had told him, several times over, that Martin's chili was the best there was. He had had the pleasure of trying it once so far and Cam had to agree. The food was absolutely delicious and, on a cold night like tonight, just what the doctor ordered.

Cam closed his eyes and settled back into the couch. The everyday sounds of the fire station helped to drain the last vestiges of tension from his body, but he couldn't help wondering what Michael was doing tonight and hoped his mate was safe wherever he was.

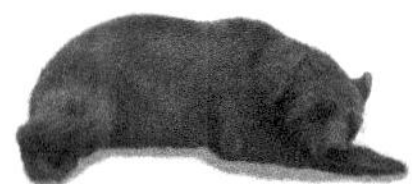

ichael felt restless, his skin itched, and his bear was pissed at him for running from his mate, even if Michael had thought he'd had a good reason. It had only been a couple of hours since he'd met his mate and Michael's life had been turned upside down. As much as he might have wanted to stay in the forest and be forgotten about, that didn't happen.

Patricia had sent her son Julius after him once it got well and truly dark out.

It hadn't taken Julius long to track him down and tell him to get his ass back home again. Julius had looked semi-amused as he'd delivered the message, before quickly shifting back into his bear form. Michael had delayed as long as he possibly could before giving in and returning to the Packard home.

He felt miserable about what he had done and hated himself even more because all he had been thinking about for the last several hours had been the fireman in the bulky bright yellow protective gear. He should have been thinking about how he had managed to almost burn down the house of the only people who had been kind to him. Instead, he was thinking with his dick and wondering what it would be like to finally, maybe, if he was lucky and the man decided Michael might be worth the trouble, feel what it was like to orgasm at the hands of someone else.

Patricia had scolded him when he'd returned with his proverbial tail between his legs. Not about the kitchen. No, for running and staying out so late and making her worry. George hadn't been angry with him about the kitchen fire either, just upset that he'd run off. Both worried over him as he sat with them in the living room. Michael looked around the house, hoping, even though he knew it was ridiculous, that his mate might still be there waiting for him. The man had probably taken one look at what a complete idiot Michael was and run in the other direction.

His shoulders slumped when he didn't find his mate waiting for him. He knew it was too much to hope for. Patricia must have noticed and walked over to give him a brief hug.

"I have a message for you," she said kindly. Why the woman wasn't spitting mad at him, Michael would never know, but he was grateful she wasn't.

"Oh?"

"A very hunky fireman by the name of Cameron Marsh asked me to let you know that the only reason he's not standing here waiting for you right now is because he has a job he takes very seriously."

Michael's heartbeat sped up. Could his mate really want to be with him?

"Really?" Michael asked, a little breathless.

"Yes. He's on shift for forty-eight hours, and he said he would be here as soon as he got off work."

Two days? Really? Who worked for that long without getting any time off? Michael's shoulders slumped again. It sounded more like an excuse for this Cameron to stay as far away from him as possible. Michael nodded soberly and went to walk away, but Patricia halted him. She gently took his chin in her hand and lifted his face until Michael looked her in the eyes.

"Firemen work in rotations. Twenty-four hours on, forty-eight hours off, or forty-eight on and seventy-two off. Cameron sounds like a very responsible young man. You should have seen his face when he had to walk away and go back to work without getting the opportunity to talk to you." Patricia's eyes narrowed and Michael knew he was being scolded for taking off like he had—again.

"I'm sorry," he whispered.

Patricia nodded at him before her expression softened again. "Give him a chance. He seems like a very nice man."

Michael bobbed his head, not sure what else to do. His throat was tight at the thought of his mate actually wanting him. He didn't know what the hell to do with a mate. As much as Michael had dreamed about this day and finally finding someone who might actually want him, now that it was here, he was scared shitless.

This is too soon. Much too soon. I'm supposed to have my life in order when I meet my mate. Except he didn't. Wasn't even close to having his life together.

He wasn't a catch by any stretch of the imagination—no education, no job, and no means to support himself. The only thing he did have going for him was his ability to start kitchen fires. Big ones. Not exactly a huge selling point in his favor, especially because his mate was a damn firefighter.

Michael headed for his room. He needed some time to think and come to terms with what had happened, both the good and the bad.

Before he'd taken two steps, Patricia called out to him. "Pack a bag, would you, honey?"

Oh god, they were kicking him out? He had thought them wanting him to come back to the house after everything was odd. He should've known that they didn't really want him. How they could kick him out after being so nice to him was a special kind of torture his father hadn't even stooped to. Michael's shoulders slumped as he nodded his head.

Patricia sighed and walked over to where he'd stopped.

"We can't stay here until we get the all clear from the fire inspector, and he won't be out here to look things over until tomorrow morning," she said calmly before she pulled him into a hug. "You're not being kicked out or punished for an accident. We're all going to stay at Christian's house for the night."

"Oh. Ooh. Okay. I'm sorry."

She sighed and hugged him harder, which caused

Michael to smile slightly. This woman really was something special.

Michael felt like crap the following morning. He'd barely slept. Every time he closed his eyes, all he could see and smell was fire. He swore he still felt the intense heat of the flames on his skin. Good thing he was a shifter or he would've been a lot worse off. Even after showering twice, Michael smelled of smoke and burnt wood. The odor clung to him as a reminder of how spectacularly he failed.

Vincent told him he smelled fine, not a hint of smoke, but Michael knew better.

The fires were larger in his dreams, hotter, and Michael was trapped, the flames getting ever closer to him as he stood too scared to move. He had bolted upright in bed several times, refusing to close his eyes again after he'd dreamed his mate burning alive. Instead he'd sat on his temporary bed with his legs pulled up to his chest for the rest of the night, too afraid to close his eyes for what he would imagine next.

When the morning light shone brightly through the curtains into his room, Michael decided it was time to move. He'd been doing a lot of thinking as he sat and waited for the night to pass. It was stupid, he knew that, but he had to see his mate, make sure the man was alive and well. Michael showered and dressed quickly, hoping he could catch Patricia, ask for her advice, and her help on an idea he had forming.

Patricia was sitting at the kitchen table with the morning paper, eating a slice of toast, her cup of coffee already empty. Michael winced at the sight of the perfect kitchen and remembered the way Patricia's had looked as they'd left the previous night—the blackened and charred walls above the stove and over the sink, the bubbled and warped countertops, the remnants of what had once been a beautiful Christmas wreath, and the tattered curtains that had hung on either side of the window.

Michael tried not to dwell on it too much. He didn't know what else he could say but *sorry*, and George and Patricia had already forgiven him. Still, he kept waiting for them to get mad like his father would've. How they could pat him on the back and smile at him, telling him not to worry was confusing.

Nice, but confusing and a bit worrying too.

He walked over to the carafe sitting on the counter, picked it up, and carried it back to the table to refill Patricia's cup. One thing he had learned in the small amount of time he had been there was how much the ex-Alpha loved her coffee.

Patricia smiled warmly up at him. "Thanks, honey." She looked at him closely and frowned. "You look tired. Did you get enough sleep last night?"

"You're welcome." Michael grinned wanly and shrugged before he went back to the kitchen and placed the carafe back on the warmer.

He didn't want to tell her he'd barely gotten any sleep. Patricia already had enough on her plate to worry about thanks to him. She didn't need more. He made himself some toast with honey—yes, he knew it was terribly cliché, but he really did love the sweet syrup—and poured himself a glass of juice, not liking coffee at all, then walked back to the table to sit down with Patricia.

After several bites of his breakfast, he noticed Patricia wasn't dressed in her normal work clothes. Instead, she wore a long-sleeved T-shirt that had definitely seen better days. Michael knew it was one of her favorites, and he guessed she also had on a pair of jeans. Definitely not work attire.

"You not going to work today?" he asked.

She stopped reading and smiled fondly at him. "No, I'm taking the day off. I have the insurance man coming out to inspect the damage, as well as the fire inspector to let us know if the building is safe for us to occupy."

Michael winced.

"Now none of that, young man. You've apologized and that's enough. It was an accident, and I don't want to hear any more about it. You hear me?" Her tone brooked no argument, and Michael wasn't stupid enough to try. She could be scary as shit when she wanted to be. But not his father kind of scary. Not really.

"I understand."

"Good, now, once the insurance man is all done, I plan on going and looking at some kitchen designs. Would you like to come with me?"

"Um… Well… I was kinda hoping you might be able to help me with something," Michael stammered, his cheeks flushing slightly.

"Oh? What did you have in mind?"

Michael told her about his idea, and Patricia beamed at him.

"I think that sounds like a wonderful idea." She reached over and patted Michael's hand, making that hard knot in his chest loosen a bit.

Mothers really do know how to fix anything.

MICHAEL COULDN'T BELIEVE HOW NERVOUS HE FELT AS he stood out front of the fire station. In the car on the opposite side of the road, Patricia waited for him to go inside. He was thankful she planned on sticking around for a little bit, in case this blew up in his face, but on the other hand, Michael didn't really want her to witness his humiliation if it didn't go the way he wanted.

He shivered as a cold gust of air whipped up, his hair flying in every direction. Michael couldn't exactly tame it as he held a bag in one hand and a thermos in the other. He took a deep breath and walked forward. Michael rang the buzzer on the door situated next to the large glass-paned hanger doors and waited for someone to let him in. He stepped back, watching through the glass as a buff guy wearing what looked to be a fireman's uniform walked toward him.

The door opened. "Hi, can I help you with something?"

"I hope so. I was wondering if Cameron Marsh was available?"

"He should be here somewhere. He didn't go out

on the call this morning. Come inside while I page him for you."

The man held the door open for Michael as he walked into the large area. The warmth of the building surrounded him the second he stepped through the door. The bays were filled with fire engines of all shapes and sizes, and equipment was stacked neatly and hung in lockers along one wall. There were men on the other side of the room polishing one of the trucks. Soft Christmas music played on the radio in the background.

Michael stood back to wait as the man picked up a phone hanging on the wall and started talking a moment later.

"Evan is going to find him and send him right over," he said as he hung up the phone.

"Thanks." Michael stood there, not sure what to do as he waited, so he continued to look around, taking everything in. He'd never been inside a fire station before and found it fascinating.

He really didn't know if he was doing the right thing or not. Hell, he didn't even know if firemen were allowed visitors while at work. Michael just knew he really wanted to see his mate, and hopefully this time not act like a complete tool but actually talk to the man. He bit his thumbnail, a nervous habit he'd had since he was a kid, and the food bag rattled as he moved.

What would he do if Cameron got angry at him for coming to his workplace? Michael knew this was probably a bad idea and was just about to tell the guy not to worry about it and leave when a door at the back of the large bay swung open and in walked the most stunning vision Michael had ever seen.

"What'd ya need, Adam..." Cameron trailed off as he came to a halt halfway into the room, his gaze locked with Michael's.

He swallowed the lump in his throat. The man was fucking breathtaking. Dark blue pants molded to his legs; a tight black shirt clung to his upper body and wrapped around the muscles of his arms. Fuck, Michael could see the ripples of his six-pack through the material. His mouth filled with saliva, and Michael had a hard time not drooling right there in the middle of the station.

What would that beard feel like against his skin? Would it be prickly or soft? The heat in the stare directed his way nearly brought Michael to his knees. No one had ever looked at him like that in his life.

"Michael." The word seemed almost choked out.

"Hi," he said, still not sure if he was doing the right thing or not. Michael looked behind him to the door, checking how much distance there was for him to cover.

"Don't go," Cameron said quickly as he hastened his steps and stopped just in front of Michael.

"Um... I brought you some lunch... Sorry... Stupid idea. You've probably already eaten. I don't really know what I'm doing here. I bet I'm not even supposed to be here. Sorry... Um... I'll just go. You can have this if you want it. I'm not sure I could actually eat anything right now anyway." Michael couldn't have stopped the verbal diarrhea if he'd wanted to. He'd just opened his mouth with no idea what he was going to say, and then it had all come tumbling out.

A small laugh that tried to hide behind a cough caused them both to look. Michael saw the guy, Adam, he thought Cameron had called him, sitting at the desk, his eyes bright, hand covering his mouth, trying hard to hold in the laugh.

"He's cute," Adam said after a moment when he had himself together again.

Michael swallowed the sudden lump in his throat. He *really* hadn't thought this through properly. What if Cameron wasn't out at work? His heart started to race as he realized just how much trouble he might have caused his mate.

Cameron grinned widely. "I'm well aware."

His mate turned back to Michael and inhaled deeply. He watched in fascination as the man's large chest expanded and contracted with the move. Cameron groaned, the sound equal parts wistful and frustrated. Michael calmed a little at his mate's reaction.

"Oh, man, you brought me pulled pork?"

Michael nodded, not sure his brain was functioning enough to formulate any more words.

"For the record, this was a fantastic idea, not stupid. I am allowed visitors; however, I might have to leave at the drop of a hat if a call comes. I haven't had lunch yet, so this is a wonderful surprise, and I can't tell you how pleased I am that you stopped by." Cameron lowered his voice and dropped his head to whisper in Michael's ear. "I've been going out of my mind since yesterday."

Cameron placed a light kiss on the skin of Michael's neck before he pulled back and stood up straight.

He reached out lightly and touched Michael's cheek, just under his eyes. "You look tired. Everything okay?"

Michael shivered at the intimate touch. He noticed the shit-eating grin Cameron wore at the effect he had on Michael, which just caused him to blush.

"Everything's fine, just a couple of nightmares last night." Michael tried to shrug it off, but frown lines appeared on Cameron's forehead.

"About the fire?" he asked quietly.

Michael nodded.

"Come here." Cameron pulled Michael into his arms and held him close for a minute. "They're just nightmares and can't hurt you. What happened yesterday could have happened to anyone and often does. It'll be all right."

Michael let out a deep breath and relaxed against his mate before he remembered where he was. He reluctantly stepped away.

"Come on, I'm starving," Cameron said then placed his hand on the small of Michael's back and led them through the bay toward the door he had walked in from.

Michael looked out the front window and was pleased to see Patricia drive off. He had his phone. She'd said to give her a call when he was finished and wanted to be picked up.

"Sorry, if it was warmer, we could go out back and sit at the picnic tables and have a little privacy. As it is, it's either on the ground in the truck bay or in the communal area at the tables in there. Either place there won't be much, if any, privacy."

"That's okay," Michael said, not entirely sure he would know what to do if they did have privacy. "The communal area is fine."

He wasn't sure how well someone of Cameron's size would do sitting on the ground to eat. Easier if they stuck with the chairs and tables. Also made it less likely for him to screw up and embarrass himself in front of his mate.

Michael looked all around as Cameron led him through the station. He'd never been in one before and the place was fascinating. His mate must have seen him looking as he smiled.

"If we have some time after lunch, I'll show you around."

"Sure," Michael said as he bobbed his head.

They walked down a long hall with doors leading off left and right until they reached the end. The room they stepped into was huge. There were two long wooden tables, both with wood benches running down their lengths. Michael guessed they could easily seat a dozen or more people per table. On the right-hand side of the room was a large kitchen. Two double-door fridges stood at the end, and a long island counter ran parallel to the one against the wall. There was someone standing at the counter with what looked like a production line of sandwiches in progress.

Tinsel draped over framed photos of the fire station from years long passed. Ornaments had been hung from the roof, the ceiling tiles keeping them in place. A *Season's Greetings* banner was strung up on the wall behind the television and in the corner by the window, a small tree with flashing colored lights sat, a couple of wrapped packages adorning the ground beneath its branches.

"None for me, thanks, Pierce," Cameron called over to the man as he led Michael to the table. He placed the thermos and bag of food down, shuffling nervously.

Pierce looked up at them. "What you got for lunch?"

Cameron waggled his eyebrows and grinned. "Smells like pulled pork to me."

"Oh man, no fair," someone said from the couches to the left as they stood and came to investigate.

Michael wasn't sure what to do, so he sat on one of the benches and started removing all the food he had brought. It might have looked like a lot, but there really wasn't that much. Certainly not enough to share with everyone. As shifters, he and Cameron tended to eat more than most people, and by the size of his mate, Michael had assumed the man ate way more than he did.

"Do we need utensils?" Cameron asked as he stood at the end of the table and watched Michael as he unpacked the food. The heavenly aromas wafted over Michael as he removed the containers from the bag.

"Plates, forks, and some cups for the hot chocolate would be great," Michael said and smiled shyly up at Cameron.

"You got it."

Michael turned and watched the man walk toward the kitchen. His ass encased in those blue pants looked like perfection.

Cameron must have felt his stare as he turned around and grinned wickedly at him. Michael blushed and turned back to what he was doing. He removed the four foil-wrapped pulled pork sandwiches and the tubs of coleslaw and mac and cheese, then set them out on the table waiting for his mate to return with the plates.

"You got a spare?" One of the firefighters came up and leaned over the table. "That smells awesome."

"Sorry." Michael shrugged.

"Evan Hawkins," he said and held out his hand. "We met briefly yesterday."

He blushed again. "Michael McKenna, sorry about that."

Evan chuckled. "It happens, man. More often than you would think."

"Hey, clear out and leave my lunch alone," Cameron said as he came back and shooed his crewmember away.

Evan laughed and reluctantly left. "If you have a spare, just yell out and I'll be right back faster than you can say *pulled pork*."

Cameron laughed and sat down. "Not gonna happen, man." He shook his head as he grinned, then passed a plate, fork, and cup to Michael. "Thanks for this. It really was a wonderful surprise."

"Y-you're welcome." Michael handed his mate a couple of sandwiches and then took one for himself.

They were quiet for a moment as they dished out their sides and each unwrapped their first sandwich.

Michael watched in fascination as Cameron took his first bite. The bread was stuffed to nearly overflowing with pork. The sounds coming from the big, buff firefighter went right through Michael, his body reacting, causing things south to sit up and take notice.

As soon as Cameron had finished his first bite, the man lifted the sandwich and took another. Michael seemed caught in some sort of trance because his mate was over halfway through his sandwich when he looked up and Michael realized he hadn't taken a single bite of his own lunch.

He had known the sandwiches were good. Just not mouth-watering near orgasmic good. Not until his mate ate one. He'd been eating at the Hungry Bear most of his life. Not only was the name of the place awesome, but so was the food. Watching Cameron eat it was almost a religious experience.

"You going to eat that or just sit there holding it all day?" Cameron nodded in the direction of his sandwich, and Michael blushed again at being caught staring. He looked away and took a bite of his food. God, so good.

They lapsed into silence again for a little while as they ate, the food disappearing quickly between the two of them. Michael was right. Cameron ate the majority of the food. He picked up his mug with the hot chocolate and took a sip before looking at the other man.

"So, how long have you been in town?" he asked hesitantly.

Michael really didn't think the middle of a firehouse surrounded by Cameron's workmates was a good time to play the get-to-know you game, but he wanted to know something, no matter how inane it might be.

But his mate smiled at him as he wiped his hands and face on a couple of the napkins Michael had brought. He reached over and picked a stray breadcrumb missed in the cleanup from Cameron's beard. The facial hair was a lot softer than Michael had expected; he'd thought it would be coarse and wiry. He was wrong.

"Thanks."

Michael nodded and smiled at his mate as he packed up all the trash and stuffed it back in the bag.

"I've only been in town for a couple of weeks," Cameron finally answered. "Between taking possession of the house I purchased and organizing the delivery of all my furniture, then setting up my home and work, I haven't had much time for anything else. What about you? What do you do?"

Michael stilled. He fiddled with the thermos in front of him as he stared down at the tabletop.

"I should probably get going," he said as he stood up.

Cameron looked momentarily shocked, but then he seemed to snap out of it as he stood as well. Michael stepped out from the bench he had been sitting on and picked up the bag of trash and the thermos.

"Here, let me get rid of that," his mate said as he reached out for the bag. His fingers made contact with Michael's arm about halfway up, making his breath catch.

Cameron lightly trailed them down and tangled with Michael's fingers fleetingly before he took possession of the bag.

"Any leftovers?" Evan called from the couch, eating a sandwich.

"Nah, man." Cameron patted his belly. "It was great. Maybe next time." Cameron looked in Michael's direction and said, "Then again, maybe not."

He grinned wickedly at his crewmember.

Evan swore at him good-naturedly, then turned back to what he was watching on the television.

Cameron nodded toward the hall. "Come on, I'll show you out."

Michael had the thermos clutched in his hand as his mate once again placed his palm on the small of Michael's back and led him back down the hallway.

"Thank you again for stopping by and surprising me."

"Happy to," he answered quietly.

"I don't know about you, but the thought of having to wait to see you again was driving me nuts."

"R-really?"

Cameron looked around to make sure they were alone before he opened a door to their right and guided Michael inside. The room was dark; even with his heightened senses, it was hard for Michael to make anything out. If not for the light from the hallway before Cameron closed the door, he would have no idea that he was currently standing in what amounted to a utility closet.

Michael didn't move. He didn't know what he was supposed to do. The door clicked closed behind them, then heat coiled at his back. Cameron stepped up and wrapped his arms around Michael's waist. The rough chuckle in Michael's ear when his mate's hands connected with the thermos he was clutching had Michael shivering. Cameron took it from him and leaned away for a moment. Michael heard the distinct sound of it being put down.

He still didn't move.

Cameron once again pressed against his back, the heat from his body making it through the layers Michael wore. Large hands pressed against his stomach, drawing Michael closer in against Cameron. He jumped slightly when he felt the soft scratch of his mate's beard against the side of his neck. Moist lips pressed to his skin before moving on, only to repeat the process.

"I honestly had no idea if I was going to survive another twenty-four hours here knowing you were out there and I hadn't had the opportunity to talk to you. You were so close, yet so far away from me all at the same time." Another kiss landed on his neck, and Michael thought his entire body was going to go up in flames at any moment.

He tilted his head back, leaning it against the hard, muscled chest of his mate. Michael moaned at the sensations shooting through his body. The large splayed hands on his abdomen pressed his back harder against Cameron. He felt the impressive rigid length against his ass and groaned at the thought of what his mate planned to do with it.

"I know our lunch setting wasn't exactly conducive to first-date talk and getting to know each other, but I will learn everything there is to know about you, Michael."

That made him snap out of the haze he was in. Michael stiffened. "I have to go."

He didn't want Cameron to know everything there was to know about him. His mate would walk away if he did, and Michael really didn't want that. For the first time in his life, he had someone who wanted him, was interested in him, and Michael didn't want to ruin that by telling Cameron that Michael was a loser with no future.

His mate pulled back, but only enough to allow him to turn around, before he wrapped one arm around Michael's back and held him close again.

Cameron cupped Michael's face with his other hand, his thumb caressing his cheek. Michael could barely see the outline of the man in front of him. He felt it, though, when Cameron stilled for a moment before he leaned down and their lips pressed together for the first time. The sensation of his mate's beard was different, not as scratchy as he'd thought it would be, but not altogether unpleasant. Michael closed his eyes as he tilted his head up for better access.

The heady scent of his mate only served to enhance Michael's libido, the smell of arousal thick on the air between them. Cameron's lips pressed firmly against his own before the man moaned and seemed to lose the tight grip he had on his control.

Michael gasped as he found himself picked up with a hand on his ass, spun around, and pressed up against the door. Cameron's mouth took his in a savage kiss, their tongues tangling together as they both tried their hardest to taste one another. The hand on his ass squeezed, and Michael moaned and thrust up, one leg wrapped around Cameron's waist, the other dangling above the floor. Michael's arms were wrapped around his mate's neck, holding on best he could.

The deep grunts and groans from Cameron were a heady thing for Michael, knowing he was the cause of them.

Sounds from outside the room had them both breaking apart. Cameron didn't let him down, just continued to hold him, their foreheads pressed together as they both breathed heavily.

Whoever was outside moved on and there was once again silence. Michael ran his fingers through the hair on the back of his mate's head.

Cameron leaned forward and placed a gentle kiss against his lips. "You're going to be the death of me. I now have to say goodbye to you again and deal with the extremely uncomfortable situation I have going on in my pants before any of my coworkers see me."

Michael chuckled nervously. "Um… Sorry?"

His mate shared in the laugh for a moment before kissing him once again and stepping back, slowly lowering Michael to the ground. "No you're not." He took Michael's hand and handed him the thermos. "Come on, I should probably get you out of here before I forget I'm at work and take you right here and now."

"In a supply closet?" Michael asked. Not exactly the most romantic of settings for their first time together. The smell of some of the cleaning products on the shelves was particularly overwhelming to his senses. If he hadn't been so distracted, Michael would have complained about it earlier.

Cameron chuckled. "As hot as what we just did was, I would never do that to you. You're my mate and deserve more than a quick romp in a dark closet. When I do finally get you under me, it will be in a bed where I can love on you and take my time getting to know every inch of your body."

Michael gulped, liking the sound of that. Before he could gather his thoughts to respond, his mate opened the door, and once he appeared sure the coast was clear, they stepped out and headed to the exit.

Cameron walked him outside. Even though it was early afternoon, the sun was hiding behind a thick layer of clouds, causing the already cold day to feel even colder. His mate cupped his cheek again and placed one last gentle kiss to Michael's lips. The beard tickled Michael before he pulled away.

"My shift ends at four tomorrow afternoon. I'll come 'round as soon after that as possible. I have a meeting with Christian about being in his territory at four thirty. So it might be closer to five thirty by the time I can get there."

"I'll see you then," he said as he smiled. Michael's body was still thrumming with the desire and heat from their all too brief encounter in the supply room. He couldn't wait to get to do it again.

He hoped Christian gave his mate permission to be in the Packard territory. The man was definitely a bear, but not one he had come across before. He could smell it.

"Thank you again for today," Cameron said.

"You're welcome." Michael was about to pull out his phone and send Patricia a message when he noticed her car parked just down from where she had dropped him off. He gave a hesitant smile to Cameron, then turned and walked toward his ride, the thermos clutched in his hand.

He looked back at the station when he reached the car and frowned when he saw his mate standing out in the cold in nothing but his work uniform. Even as bears, they still were susceptible to very low temperatures, and today's was getting down there. As it was, Michael shivered in the jacket he wore. He smiled and waved one last time at Cameron. His mate smiled and nodded back, his hands stuffed in his uniform pants. Michael tore his gaze away and got in the car, the hot air from the vehicle's heater immediately surrounding him.

"So, how did it go?"

5

Questions flew in Cam's direction once Michael had left. Everyone wanted to know why Michael was there and why he was bringing Cam lunch at the station. When he'd been interviewed for the job, he told the Chief that he was gay and was told that Cam's personal life was of no concern to him. Cam had wanted to keep things quiet while he settled in and got to know everyone better, but Michael had taken that choice off the table.

Not that Cam was complaining. When he'd made that decision, Cam hadn't had anyone in his life. Now that he'd met his mate, Cam wanted to claim the man and make Michael his, and there was no way he would deny Michael ever, even if his workmates didn't like it.

"Why was Micky McKenna here?" Martin asked.

Micky?

"Why are you so special you get lunch delivered?" Tyler followed up.

"Dude, you move fast." Evan grinned and held his fist out for Cam to pound.

Man, small towns where everyone knew everyone did not change no matter what state a person lived in.

Cam shook his head and chuckled, but pounded Evan's fist anyway. He looked around the room. The majority of the guys were still gathered, only Pierce and Mark having gone. Cam took a deep breath and bit the bullet, deciding it was best to just get it out there and then get back to work.

"I'm gay," he said confidently. Cam wasn't ashamed of who he was. He just didn't believe who he slept with was anyone's business except for him and who he dated. "Michael is my...*partner*."

He didn't miss the confused look Evan gave him. He didn't blame the guy. Cam had only met Michael yesterday, and Evan had been there for the meeting. But how do you explain to a room full of humans who knew nothing about shifters that he'd met his soul mate and was falling for the man hard and fast?

Cam looked around the room, sure to make eye contact with each and every one of his colleagues. A couple didn't look exactly happy at his news. "If you have a problem with any of that, you're more than welcome to seek me out and talk things through or you can always talk to the chief. He knows I'm gay and hired me because I'm good at my job. Who I sleep with has absolutely no bearing on my ability to fight fires."

When he was finished, Cam turned and left the room, heading to Chief Walker's office. He thought he better give the man a heads-up.

. . .

A WORK SHIFT HAD NEVER LASTED SO LONG IN CAM'S life. Even though it was only forty-eight hours, with everything that had happened, it felt like he'd been stuck at work for a week or more. Now he was finally free and he wasn't due back until Christmas Eve. Thankfully that was only a twenty-four hour shift and not a forty-eight. That meant he would still be able to spend some time on Christmas with his new mate.

His parents and siblings had wanted Cam to come back to Montana to celebrate the holiday with family, but they understood why he couldn't. It just wasn't good practice to start a new job and two weeks later go on vacation. Besides, those types of things were planned well in advance. Cam was the newbie at the station, and he didn't mind taking the shifts that would pull others away from their kids and families on special occasions. Although, now that he had Michael, that might change a little after he'd put in his time and was no longer bottom of the barrel.

Cam slung his bag over his shoulder as he said goodbye to the guys and walked out the station doors. Since his announcement the previous day, things were a little strained with a couple of the guys, but the others didn't seem to have a problem and treated him just as they had before Michael's visit.

He pulled his keys from his jeans pocket and clicked the button to unlock the doors. He loved his baby, had purchased it just before he'd left Montana and had driven it all the way here. The 2014 Chevy Silverado dual cab truck in metallic blue drove like a dream and had pulled his old and well-loved custom Harley behind it. Cam didn't get to ride his bike anywhere near as much as he would like to, but as soon as the weather permitted, he would be out there on it once again.

Firefighters weren't paid a fortune, but Cam had been scrimping and saving for years. He'd lived at home well past the time when most of his friends had all moved out on their own. His parents owning a ranch with plenty of room helped. He'd worked there on his days off from the station, earning him a second wage. Cam'd done that for more years than he cared to count. He'd yet to find a second job since he'd moved to Gatlinburg, wanting to take a little time to settle in first. Cam didn't think it would take too much longer before all the free time got to him and he started looking.

Although with Michael in his life now, he might hold off for a while.

Cam threw his duffle on the passenger seat, then started the truck and cranked the heat, not because he was overly cold, but he needed to be able to see out his windows. While he waited, Cam entered the details for Christian's house into the GPS on his phone. When his view was finally clear, he pulled out of the parking lot and followed the directions to the Alpha's house.

Meeting new Alphas always sucked. They seemed to assume that with his size, he would naturally want to lead and therefore were never friendly toward him. It had taken his Alpha back home a long time to understand that Cam wanted nothing to do with leading the sleuth. After meeting Patricia Packard the other day, he had quiet hopes that her son might be different. Patricia had been wary of him at first, but it hadn't taken long for the ex-Alpha to warm up to him.

Shortly after leaving the station, he pulled up in front of nice single-story house not far from where his mate was living.

Cam turned off the truck and got out. The colder temperature immediately caused his skin to break out in goose bumps. He should have thrown on a jacket, but Cam had been in such a rush to leave work and get this meeting over with that he had completely forgotten all about one. He couldn't wait to see his mate again.

He locked his truck, shoved his hands in his pockets, and made his way up the paved walk to the door. The closer he got to the house, the more his body started to react. His bear sat up and growled, clawing to get out, to shift, to claim what was theirs. Cam paused as he stood in front of the door and inhaled deeply.

His body thrummed as the incredibly sexy scent of his mate washed over him. Michael was here. Cam quickly rang the bell. Twenty-four hours was far too long to go without seeing or even talking to his man. Cam had never once questioned the job he had chosen for himself years ago. Now that he'd met Michael, he was wondering how he could possibly go forty-eight hours at a time without seeing his mate.

The door opened and he was faced with a short, slightly pudgy man with wavy light brown hair and green eyes.

"Ah… Hi. Cameron Marsh. I have a meeting with Christian Packard." Cam held out his hand and the short man immediately took it, his grip firmer than Cam expected.

"Vincent Marsden, Christian's mate," Vincent said as he let go and stepped back. "Please, come in."

"Thanks." Cam walked inside, the house lovely and warm. He looked around, searching, but not seeing anything of his surroundings except the man that sat in the living room on a couch. "Michael."

His mate looked at him immediately when he heard his name, Michael smiling hesitantly as he stood. Cam knew it was rude, but he ignored his host and made his way to his mate.

When he was stopped in front of Michael, Cam cupped his face, then tilted his head up and bent down to gently kiss him. His mate seemed to melt under his touch, relaxing in his grip. Cam wasn't so far gone as to forget completely where he was or what he was doing there, so he kept the kiss gentle and sweet, soft lips pressed against his own with only the barest hint of tongue coming out to play.

His bear was less understanding.

Reluctantly Cam ended the kiss but refused to let go of his mate. He pulled him in close until Michael's head rested against his shoulder and the man's arms wrapped around his waist. The joy and contentment he felt at having this man so close to him was almost overwhelming.

"You still look tired," he murmured as he ran his thumb under Michael's eye.

"I had another bad night."

Cam didn't like that Michael seemed to be having nightmares; he could see the strain starting to show on his face, and dark circles had started forming under his mate's beautiful eyes. He'd give anything to be able to help his mate through this.

"Missed you," he whispered.

God, his parents had told him the mating pull was strong, but Cam had had no idea it would feel like this. He felt settled and relaxed for the first time since meeting Michael, knowing they had some time to get to know one another before Cam had to go back to work. Hopefully Michael would let Cam claim him before then, and his bear wouldn't be such a grouch at being separated. He could hope at least.

"Hmm…missed you, too."

"What are you doing here? Not that I'm not very happy to see you." Cam didn't want his mate to get the impression that Cam didn't want him there; he just hadn't been expecting him.

"Christian's a good man, and Patricia told me that as your mate, my place is by your side."

"Thank you for that, Micky, and my mother is correct," Christian said calmly. "Mates belong together."

Cam hadn't even heard Christian come up behind them, he was so wrapped up in Michael. He kissed the top of his mate's head, then looked down at him.

"Micky?" he asked because several people had called him that since his mate's visit to the station. "Do you want me to call you that instead of Michael?"

"I prefer Michael. Micky is someone I don't want to be anymore."

Cam stared at his mate for a minute wondering what that comment meant, but now wasn't the time to ask. Instead he simply nodded, gave his mate a gentle kiss on the tip of his nose, and then chuckled when Michael scrunched up his face.

Cam turned to face the man who had spoken earlier. He kept hold of his mate, one arm wrapped around Michael's waist, holding him close. Christian stood in the entrance to the living room. The Alpha was tall, at least three or four inches above Cam's own height of six three. His thick black hair and the dark stubble on his face matched with the piercing blue eyes and the muscled body just screamed Alpha to Cam. The suit he wore helped with the image; Cam could practically feel the power radiating from this man.

"Christian Packard. Welcome to our neck of the woods." The Alpha indicated that they should take a seat on the couch.

He sat with Michael snuggled next to him. "Thank you. Cameron Marsh. But everyone calls me Cam."

Christian walked into the room and took a seat in one of the large recliners opposite them. Vincent walked over and took a seat on the armrest of Christian's chair. The Alpha immediately reached out and wrapped his arm around his mate, holding him.

Cam smiled at the easy touches between the two men. He was surprised to find an Alpha with a male mate right in the middle of Tennessee. They didn't hide their relationship, although they were behind closed doors right now. Cam wondered if they were just as open when they were out in public.

"So, Cam, what brings you to the great state of Tennessee?" Christian asked.

"Work. I took a job with the Gatlinburg fire department. Moved here from Montana, the rest of my family is still there."

"And you wanted to seek my permission to use our lands to shift and run?"

"I did. I was also going to ask if it was possible to petition to join the sleuth. I don't much like the idea of being a lone bear," Cam informed him. He liked the connection he felt when he was part of a group. The two weeks he'd been here already without anyone to lean on or talk to or even somewhere he could shift and run was weighing on him.

"Well, seeing as how you've met your mate, I'm assuming you're not planning on leaving anytime soon?"

Cam shook his head. "Not in the near future, no."

"Then I see no reason why you can't be granted admittance to the sleuth as a mate to one of our members." Christian grinned.

He felt himself relax. Cam hadn't even realized he'd been so tense, worried over what the big Alpha would do or say. It helped that Christian was so big. He probably didn't see Cam as a threat to his position.

"Grizzly if I'm not mistaken, correct?"

"Correct." It wasn't often people could tell what type of bear he was. Their shifter numbers were almost as low as the numbers of the animals in the wild.

"We'll have to be careful that you're not spotted. Grizzlies aren't found in this area." Christian looked thoughtful for a moment, and Cam worried the man might decide he was too much of a risk for the rest of the sleuth. But the man didn't say anything more on the topic.

"I'll be careful, the last thing I want to do is put any of the sleuth members in danger, especially my mate."

Christian nodded in understanding and smiled. He stood and held his hand out for Cam.

He took it.

"Welcome to the sleuth, Cam. We'll have the official swearing in at the next gathering. I'll leave it to your mate to show you where you can go for a run, and I look forward to getting to know you better."

Cam beamed. He could really get to like this man. Christian was obviously comfortable in his own skin; not once did he treat Cam with anything but kindness. There was no posturing and no need for dick measuring. Christian was Alpha and he had no doubts that he belonged in that role.

"I look forward to getting to know you, too." Cam found he meant it too. "Right now, if it's all right with you, I might take my mate and go for a run. It feels like forever since I've been able to let my bear roam free."

Michael stood beside him and Cam smiled at the younger man when he felt a hand gently slip into his own.

"That sounds like a wonderful idea. Enjoy. If you'll excuse me, I need to get out of this monkey suit and then spend some time with my own mate. I'm sure I'll see you soon enough. Seeing as how Michael is having Christmas dinner with the family, please consider yourself invited as well."

"Thank you, that's very kind. I'm working until four on Christmas Day, so it all depends on what time you are planning to eat."

"On Christmas we usually have a late breakfast, a very light lunch, and then a large dinner late in the afternoon."

"Sounds wonderful."

"It is. I'll leave the details for you two to sort out. Cam, it was a pleasure, and once again, welcome." Christian turned and looked at Michael, then smiled gently. "I'm very glad you've found your mate, Michael. I hope you'll be very happy together."

"Thanks, Christian," his mate said.

Their Alpha nodded and then left the room, no doubt going to change out of his clothes. Cam didn't blame him. If he had to wear a suit like that to work every day, Cam would want to get out of it as soon as possible as well.

They said their goodbyes to Vincent, and Michael followed Cam out to his truck. He unlocked the doors, and once they were settled inside the cab with the heater going again, Cam turned and faced his mate. Michael was looking around the inside of his truck in wide-eyed wonder. Cam smiled at just how innocent his mate seemed at that moment.

"Would you like to go for a run with me?" he asked softly, not wanting to break the peaceful silence but having to ask the question anyway.

Michael turned and grinned at him. "I'd love to."

Cam leaned over and kissed his mate. He licked

his tongue across Michael's bottom lip before his mate opened his mouth and allowed Cam entrance without question. The little noises Michael made had shots of arousal coursing through his body and heading straight for his dick. Cam had to lift his ass off the seat and adjust himself he became so uncomfortable.

He gentled the kiss after a minute and pulled back. Michael sat there, his eyes still closed, for several moments after Cam had broken the lip-lock. His mate looked stunning. Cam reached out and lightly brushed his thumb across Michael's lips to wipe away the small coating of saliva. His mate's lips were pink and a little swollen from their make-out session, and he could see a slight redness around Michael's mouth, no doubt from Cam's beard.

When Michael eventually opened his eyes, he stared at Cam through half-lidded pools of desire. He had to restrain himself from diving back over there and taking his mate right here and now. His bear was all for that course of action.

"God, you look fucking edible," Cam rasped, lust riding him hard.

Michael blushed, his cheeks turning a stunning shade of pink. Cam had to grip the steering wheel, hard, in order not to reach out and take what he wanted. He took several deep breaths, trying to calm his body down. All he managed to do was get his mate's scent well and truly ingrained in his senses.

"We going to run?" Michael asked hesitantly.

Cam nodded, not sure he could respond just then. He checked his mirrors and pulled out onto the street.

"Which way?" he asked after a moment.

Michael chuckled. "Um… Back that way."

He pointed with his thumb back over his shoulder toward where they had just come from.

Cam groaned before turning the truck around at the first opportunity. He could tell he was going to be absolutely no use to anyone until he was able to claim his mate. He just hoped it was sooner rather than later.

6

ichael sat quietly in the cab of his mate's beautiful pickup. The thing looked and smelled brand new. He wondered just how long Cam had had it and what it would be like to actually be able to afford a truck, let alone drive one. Michael had only had three driving lessons when he was younger before his father had put a stop to that. He had no idea why his dad hadn't let him get his license or finish school. The only explanation Michael could come up with was the fact the man was a bastard. Learning to drive was just something else he added to the ever-growing list of things he wanted to achieve to get his life on track.

He wondered what Cam's reaction would be when he found out that Michael couldn't even drive a car. Michael wasn't even sure if Patricia and George knew he couldn't, since the subject had never really come up. He supposed he would just have to wait and see. Cam would either help him or walk away because

Michael wasn't worth the effort. He was expecting the latter, so he'd decided to try to soak up as much time with Cam as he could before he was no longer in Michael's life.

Michael gave the directions to the parking lot their sleuth usually used to get to their meetings. He supposed he could have just directed Cam back to the Packard house and they could have taken off into the woods behind the property, but Michael wanted his mate all to himself. Patricia and George had returned to their house earlier in the day after they'd received the all clear from the inspector that morning. If they went back there, Michael wasn't sure they could escape. The woman was extremely good at extracting information from people and could have easily had a job as an interrogator for the police force.

There were a couple of other cars in the parking lot when they arrived, one, a late nineties model Ford, he recognized as belonging to an old school friend, Carson Brooks. They had been good friends before Michael dropped out. Since then they only saw each other at the gatherings and with Michael's father being the ass he was, Carson had kept his distance.

Even though his dad and older brother had been gone for a few months now, Michael hadn't yet tried to rekindle any of the friendships he'd had when he was younger, unsure of how he'd be received by any of them.

He also wanted to get his life in order first.

That plan hadn't included meeting his mate.

They got out of the pickup and Cam circled around front, holding out his hand for Michael. He smiled a little and hurried to take his mate's hand. Cam's large hand felt like it swallowed Michael's whole. His mate had calluses on his palm and the rough hard patches felt odd against his own smooth, soft skin.

Michael led them down the path that had been worn into the earth from several decades of use. The cold wind blew through the trees, and Michael thought they might be in for some snow tonight. It certainly smelled like it. The sun was well on its way down, casting muted orange beams of light in a last-ditch effort before it disappeared for the night.

When they entered the small gathering area, Michael led Cam over to where he usually changed and stored his clothes. He had a backpack he kept out here permanently so he could put his clothes away and they would be protected from the elements while he was in shifted form. He could see several little piles of clothes scattered throughout the area, letting him know that the cars in the parking lot definitely belonged to members of his sleuth.

Michael started stripping, not thinking about anything else but getting to shift and run with his mate. He'd just toed off his sneakers and shucked his jeans when he heard a low growl behind him. Michael turned too quickly, and his legs tangled in the bottom of his jeans. He windmilled his arms for a moment and then went down, landing hard on his ass in the soft grass.

"Oomph." The impact knocked the breath out of him.

Michael looked up wide-eyed, hoping against

hope that Cam for some reason or another might not have just seen him fall on his ass.

His hope was dashed when his mate stood there, his mouth slightly open, the mirth evident in his expression. He held out a hand for Michael, and carefully, once he had his legs untangled, Michael took it and pulled himself up. Cam hauled him right into his arms and kissed the tip of Michael's nose.

"You're fucking adorable. You know that?" Cam asked in a rough growl.

"Any chance you can pretend you didn't just see that?" Michael felt the heat already gathering in his cheeks. He shivered from being almost naked in the cold outdoors, but the warmth radiating from Cam helped.

"We can pretend, yes. Although some things just can't be unseen. You all right? You didn't hurt yourself, did you?" Cam pressed his hand against Michael's back and then smoothed it down until it cupped his ass cheek. He gave a gentle squeeze.

A small groan escaped Michael. Man that felt good. His mate's touches were addicting. It was going to suck if Cam decided not to claim him.

Michael stepped back and smiled when he saw the questioning expression his mate wore. "I'm getting a little cool out here, being nearly naked. Are we going to shift?"

He shivered again, but this time it had nothing to do with the weather and absolutely everything to do with the way his mate's gaze raked over his body from head to foot and back up again.

Cam took a predatory step toward him, and as

much as Michael would have loved to fall into the man's arms, they needed to talk first. He wanted Cam to know what he was getting into. Instead he pushed down his briefs and let go of the hold he had on his inner animal.

His bear roared in happiness at being let out to play. He felt his bones reshaping, fur sprung from his skin, instantly warming him against the outside temperatures, his hands and feet grew claws, and his face reshaped. It took less than thirty seconds and Michael stood on all fours as a black bear. Compared to others in his sleuth, Michael was small, he looked more like a teenager after their first shift, one that still had some growing to do. That wasn't the case, though. He was full grown, just small.

Michael stood still as Cam walked toward him, the man's expression gentle. He reached out, ran his large hand over Michael's head, and scratched behind his ear. Michael made a chuffing sound. God that felt good.

"You and I are going to have a very long talk tonight," Cam said softly, but there was no menace or heat to his words, just determination. Michael nodded his head and then Cam stepped back. "You're a very cute black bear."

He didn't know if he should be offended by the *cute* comment or not. Before he could make up his mind, his attention was diverted as Cam started stripping. He sat on his haunches and watched as what seemed like miles upon miles of lightly furred, well-muscled skin was revealed. Michael had to concentrate hard to make sure his tongue wasn't hanging out. Jesus his mate was sexy as fuck.

He couldn't break his gaze away if he had wanted to. Michael watched as Cam removed his boots and his jeans. The guy wasn't wearing a damn thing under them. Before Michael could get a good look at more than just a naked hip, Cam shifted. In less time than it had taken Michael, Cam now stood in front of him on all fours as a giant grizzly.

The stunning golden fur was almost a honey color in the dying rays of light, and the closer the fur got to the ground the darker it became. His paws were a rich caramel color, almost chocolate. The bear was also huge. Michael thought he might be as much as twice his size. If Michael didn't know that he was looking at his mate, he would have been running in the opposite direction. The large teeth he could see poking through as Cam walked closer toward him just lent credence to the scariness.

Cam paused when he stood right in front of Michael and then lowered his head and rubbed against the side of Michael's. Michael pushed back against the other bear, nuzzling. If he'd been a cat, Michael could have seen himself purring.

After several minutes of them rubbing against one another, Cam finally pulled away and they headed off into the woods. The leaf-strewn ground was soft under his paws. Happy and excited for what seemed like the first time in forever, Michael took off in a run, playing.

He could hear Cam behind him, but he didn't stop. Michael climbed on fallen tree trunks and batted at the thick layer of leaves on the ground. No mate in sight. Where did Cam hide? A bear that big shouldn't be able to disappear. All of a sudden, Michael found himself rolling, a giant grizzly bear having tackled him.

They scrambled around for a minute, Michael gaining his feet again and dancing out of the way as Cam came for him again. His mate bit him, not hard enough to break the skin or even hurt, just a little love bite. They batted at each other and played for hours, the sun having long since set. Cam definitely had the size advantage in both height and weight, and Michael constantly found himself on the ground with Cam on top of him.

After one such occasion, Michael walked over to a particularly good-looking tree and stood up against it, his back to the trunk. Oh god, that felt good. Michael moved against the tree, the bark scratching his back in all the right places. Cam sat and watched him, and if Michael didn't know better, he would swear the bear was grinning at him.

Exhausted from all the playing, Michael curled up on his side and laid his head down. His mate padded over to him, nudged him once with his nose, and then took up position behind him, his larger frame easily surrounding Michael in warmth. Cam's head came up and rested alongside Michael's. He sighed, content and happy, and he settled in and closed his eyes, satisfied to stay exactly where he was and have a little power nap before they headed back to the clearing, their clothes, and the talk that was waiting for them.

CAM SLOWLY AWOKE, THE INTOXICATING SCENT OF HIS mate surrounding him. They hadn't slept very long, just enough to recharge their batteries after their exhilarating play session. Cam had never had so much fun in his bear form before. Playing with his mate, chasing him and taking him down, had his blood pumping and his dick hard. Cam wondered if Michael would ever consent to them consummating in this form?

It was something to think about later. Before they even contemplated that, Cam wanted to claim his mate as a human.

He nuzzled up against the back of Michael's furry head, and the bear moved beneath him. Cam couldn't tell if Michael was awake or it was just a reaction to the touch. He nuzzled again, and Michael lifted his head slightly and turned to look at Cam. He wanted to kiss his mate in that moment so badly, instead he settled for leaning in and licking Michael's snout. His mate let him, then licked him back.

Soon they were once again rolling on the ground until Cam had Michael pinned beneath him.

Cam nuzzled Michael's neck one last time before he crawled backward and let his mate up. If he didn't, he was going to take Michael right there and then, and he wanted their first time together to be special, not in response to their animalistic lust.

They slowly wandered back to the clearing, Michael pushing up against his side every so often, as if the bear wanted to be as close to him as possible. Cam had no complaints about that whatsoever.

When they reached the clearing, they went straight to their pack with their clothes. Cam didn't watch his mate shift, he couldn't, too keyed up to able to see Michael naked in front of him and not want to take his mate.

Cam shifted. He would never get used to the feeling of his bones and muscles shrinking as he reformed back into his human shape. The sensation of his fur disappearing and his claws retracting was something else entirely, he had no idea how to describe it. Once Cam was again on two feet, he quickly pulled on his clothes, tucking away his aching length, hopefully before Michael could see the state he was in.

Dressed again, Michael stashed the bag back where he'd pulled it from and took the hand Cam held out to him. He pulled his mate in close, unable to resist him. Just one kiss wouldn't hurt.

He cupped the side of Michael's head and tilted it up as he bent his own down. Their lips met in a fiery kiss that felt like solar systems exploded around them. Cam pushed his tongue inside, probing, tasting, and licking. Michael wrapped his arms around Cam's neck and held on tight, their bodies pressed up close against one another. He could feel the hardness in Michael's pants against his body and groaned into his mate's mouth.

Fuck, the man was like sex on legs. All his self-control disappeared around Michael.

Eventually he pulled away, gasping for air. Cam

had to breathe deeply to get his body back under control. He was about two seconds away from sprouting claws and ripping Michael's clothes from his body. When sensations in his fingers started as his claws began to slowly extend, Cam revised his estimate to one second.

"You're too damn tempting for your own good," Cam said quietly, his voice deep and husky even to his own ears.

Michael grinned up at him and fluttered his lashes, the little minx. Cam growled and his mate chuckled.

"Come on, big guy, I'm hungry."

The mention of food had Cam's own stomach growling, letting the world know that it too needed feeding.

"Would you like to come over for dinner?" Cam asked his mate. The mere idea of Michael in his den, sitting in his living room, at his kitchen table eating with Cam, and spread out naked on Cam's bed had his body thrumming with want.

"Um… Sure, I would love to." Michael smiled at him again, and suddenly Cam couldn't get out of there fast enough.

He took Michael's hand once again and practically dragged the man back down the now dark path to the parking lot. There were two new cars in the area when they arrived, and the others that had been there had all departed at some point.

Cam unlocked his truck, and once he was certain his mate was secure, he headed back toward town and his house. The light from Michael's phone shone bright in the darkness of the cab as his mate tapped away at the keys.

"Everything all right?" he asked, not wanting to appear too nosy.

"Yeah, just letting Patricia know where I was," Michael answered as he tucked the phone back in the pocket of his pants.

"How did you come to be living with them?" he asked casually.

Even though Cam was driving, he still saw his mate stiffen in the seat beside him. He didn't like the action at all. Cam reached over and squeezed Michael's leg, trying to reassure the man as much as he could.

"Could we…maybe leave that discussion until we're at your place?" Michael asked hesitantly.

He glanced over and found his mate once again biting on his bottom lip. Michael seemed to have collapsed in on himself a little. Cam didn't like the thought that just that one question was enough to ruin the joyful mood they'd had going on. He hated to think what it could be that was so bad that would have Michael acting this way.

Cam squeezed his mate's leg again in reassurance and nodded. "Whatever you need, we're almost there." He wanted to change the subject and blurted out the first thing he could think of. "What would you like for dinner?"

Michael took his time answering. "What are my options?"

Cam considered what he had in the fridge and freezer at home. He didn't have a great deal, but he had enough to make something nice. "Chicken or salmon."

"Oh… I love salmon."

Cam grinned. "Salmon it is, then."

Michael smiled, placed his hand over Cam's, and rested it there for the rest of the journey home. When it came time to shift gears, he contemplated how difficult it would be to shift with his left hand, but finally concluded that it wasn't worth risking their lives and reluctantly pulled his hand away from Michael's.

Cam steered his truck into the drive to the small house he had bought—well, technically the bank owned it, but Cam ignored that small fact. He'd found it online while he had been in Montana and started the paperwork then. As soon as Cam had arrived in town he'd gone right there to inspect the place and settle on it. His furniture had arrived the previous week, and Cam had thankfully unpacked the last box before starting his previous work shift. He couldn't stand boxes hanging around waiting to be unpacked.

Hopefully Michael would like the place. It wasn't much, nothing fancy, just a three-bedroom, one-bath with an attached garage.

He pressed a button and the garage door opened. Cam waited patiently, then drove in and parked the pickup. He pressed the button again and the door started back down. When he shut off the truck and the lights went out, it plunged the room into darkness.

"I'll come around and get you," Cam said, then exited before Michael could reply.

He made his way around the truck in the dark. Even though Cam hadn't been there long, he'd cleared a path after the first night when he'd kicked some boxes and nearly ended up on his ass. The house was old so there were no automatic lights. He had a plan to put in a sensor, but so far hadn't gotten around to it.

Cam opened Michael's door and stood back a little to allow his mate to slide out of the cab. Michael still managed to rub up against him as he got down. Cam bit back a moan. They needed some food and to talk. His mate didn't deserve to be mauled the second Cam got him in private. He stepped back and placed a hand on Michael's back.

"The door is just over here," he said as he led his mate around the truck.

As soon as Cam opened the door, he flicked on the inside light switch. The kitchen illuminated, showing off the dated cabinetry and counters. The only thing new in the kitchen were the appliances. Cam's two-door fridge/freezer barely fit in the appointed place, and his shiny coffeemaker sat on the counter next to his kettle and toaster. Even though the kitchen was dated, it was big. A huge butcher block sat in the middle of the room, the double sink over to the right, and a large breakfast counter with four barstools stood at the opposite end, leading through to the living areas.

"Come on in. Why don't you have a seat and I'll see about getting dinner started."

"Thanks," Michael said and took a seat on one of the barstools.

Cam headed to the freezer and pulled out some salmon fillets he'd purchased the other day. He set them in the microwave to defrost, then turned back to the fridge.

"Do you like potatoes, asparagus, and carrots?" he asked as he looked in the vegetable crisper to see what he had. The potatoes were in the pantry, but most others were kept in the fridge.

"Sounds great."

Cam grabbed a couple of carrots and the bunch of asparagus, along with a lemon and a bottle of cream. Next, he took some potatoes from the pantry and started preparing the vegetables.

He worked in silence for a minute or two, his mate watching his every move. Cam liked the intimate feeling.

"So, Michael, why don't you tell me a little about yourself?" he said to make conversation and hopefully get to know his mate a little better.

Once again, his mate stiffened. "What would you like to know?"

"Well, seeing as we're in a private place and no longer surrounded by a half dozen of my work colleagues, I guess I'm interested in the hard stuff, you know…date of birth, favorite color, if you have any hobbies, family situation…if you've ever watched porn?" Cam looked up at a slight choking noise and waggled his brows. "Oh, sorry. Bad host here. Can I get you a drink?"

When Michael seemed to have recovered his ability to talk, he nodded. "A drink would be great."

"Beer okay?" Cam went to the fridge and pulled out a bottle, showing it to Michael.

"Beer's fine, thanks." His mate took the drink and Cam grabbed one for himself as well before going back to making dinner.

"So, where were we? That's right, porn." He glanced up and watched his mate intently; the pink turned to a bright red in Michael's cheeks. It was fascinating and sexy as fuck all at the same time. "I'm going to take that as a yes."

"Yes on the porn," Michael said, then took a long swallow of his beer. "What else was there? Um… Birthday, August twenty-first, 1992. Favorite color's red. I have a father and a brother still living, however I no longer talk to them—I haven't seen either one since late September—and I don't really have any hobbies. I like to read, though, if that counts."

Cam nodded. "Sure, that counts. Why haven't—"

"Is that your family?" His mate interrupted him, obviously flustered.

"Yeah." Cam didn't like Michael's reaction, but he would let him have his little distraction for now. He would get the answers out of his mate soon.

Cam looked over to the fridge where photos of his entire family were hung with magnets. He smiled. He loved his family. Cam would have to call them soon and let them know he'd met his mate. His parents would probably jump on the first plane down here so they could meet Michael right away and welcome the man into the family. Cam grinned. His mom and dad would love Michael.

Cam pointed to the pictures on the fridge. "My mom and dad, Abigail and Henry. Mom prefers Abi. My brother Joel and my two sisters Megan and Jillian."

He glanced back at Michael; the man had a sort of melancholy look to him. "They all look very happy."

"They are. They annoy the hell out of me sometimes, but they're family and I love them. They're good people."

"Where are they?" Michael asked.

"They're all back in Montana. I'm the black sheep of the family, the only one to leave."

"Funny, I could have sworn you were a brown grizzly." His mate grinned. "Maybe I need to have my eyes checked."

"Smartass." Cam chuckled as he picked up a slice of carrot and threw it across the counter. His mate easily caught it and ate the projectile.

"So why did you leave?" Michael asked before taking another sip of his beer.

"I wanted to find my mate." He shrugged.

Michael stared at him for a moment, not saying anything. Cam looked up from the vegetables he was preparing and wasn't sure about the expression on Michael's face.

"You okay?" he asked.

Michael nodded, but he didn't look okay. Cam set down the knife and walked around the counter. He turned his mate until Cam stood between his legs and cupped the man's cheeks so they were looking into each other's eyes.

"What's going on?" he asked gently.

"You...you left your entire family to look for me?"

Why did Michael sound so hesitant? Like he wasn't worth the sacrifice?

"Yeah, and I have to say, moving across the country is one of the best decisions I've ever made." Cam leant down to lightly kiss his mate and didn't miss the slight flinch Michael made at his words.

He stood back and really looked at his mate. Michael was young, he already knew that, but in that exact moment, the man looked even younger. Cam made a decision, took his mate's hand, and pulled him from the stool.

"Where are we going?" Michael asked, confused.

"Come on, we need to talk and we can do it more comfortably through here."

Cam led his mate from the kitchen and into the living room with his nice plush sofas. He indicated for Michael to take a seat while he went and lit the fire already laid out. Once he was sure the fire was burning sufficiently, he placed the grate in front of it, then turned and switched on the Christmas lights.

He hadn't had the time or the inclination this year to go out and get a real tree. Instead he had a small fake tree set up in the corner of the room. Colored lights, a few balls, and a garland of tinsel were its only adornments. If Cam's parents saw his poor excuse for a Christmas tree, they would be horrified.

Thankfully, they weren't here and he could get away with it.

The light from the fire and the strings on the tree bathed the room in their soft glow. The area soon warmed up, and Cam walked over to sit on the couch next to his mate. He tucked one leg under him and turned so he was facing Michael. He knew whatever the man was holding back wasn't going to be sunshine and roses, but whatever it happened to be, Cam would help him with it. They were mates, even if they hadn't yet completed the bond, and that meant more to Cam than just about anything else in the world.

7

Michael sat there facing Cam, the crackling of the fire the only sound in the room. He knew what was coming. Michael just wasn't sure if he was ready to spill his guts about his crappy life and his hopeless outlook for the future. The small amount of time Michael had spent with his mate wasn't enough. Michael wanted to grab onto Cam with two hands and never let go of him.

He could easily fall in love with this massive grizzly firefighter.

Cam reached out and took his hand. Michael sat there a little stunned when his mate lifted his hand and kissed his palm, the whiskers of his beard tickling Michael's soft skin. He locked gazes with Michael, his eyes gentle and kind, and Michael couldn't help but relax.

"You can tell me anything, Michael. You're my mate, and to me that means you're the most important person in my life. I would sooner cut off my right arm than hurt you."

Michael's throat clogged and his eyes started to water as he sat there staring at the man he hoped would want him.

"I don't have a job," he blurted suddenly.

Michael didn't know why that was the first thing out of his mouth, but once the dam broke, he just couldn't seem to stop.

"My mom's dead, my dad and my brother are homophobic assholes who tried to kill Christian and were banished from the sleuth. He was a controlling bastard that drank too much and liked to use his fists to make his point. I never got the chance to finish high school: Dad stopped me from going halfway through my sophomore year, not that there was much point in me continuing to go. I'd missed so much school up to that point anyway. I'm an idiot who doesn't know how to do anything. I can't drive; hell, I can't even cook a simple meal without burning down the kitchen."

By the time Michael had finished spilling his guts, he was practically hyperventilating. Oh god, why had he just done that?

Michael couldn't bear to look at Cam, instead choosing to stare at their joined hands resting against the soft leather fabric of the couch they shared. With his free hand, Michael reached up and wiped away the tears that steadily leaked from his eyes. When Cam pulled his hand away from Michael's, a small sob escaped. Michael wanted to clutch his mate's hand in his own and hold on for dear life, never letting go. He just couldn't bring himself to be even more pathetic than he already was.

When strong arms wrapped around him and pulled him in close against his mate's chest, Michael startled, not expecting the move. Cam rubbed gently along his back, Michael's head tucked in the hollow of his shoulder. Michael could hear and feel the bigger man murmuring to him, he just couldn't make out what he was saying.

Tentatively Michael wrapped his arms around the much larger man, and he fisted the warm material of Cam's shirt and held on. He cried quietly, sobbing as all the emotion he'd kept bottled up ever since his mom had died came flooding out. Michael had no idea how long they sat there. Eventually his tears stopped and he was able to get his breathing back under control.

"Shh… Everything's going to be okay." Little kisses were placed on the top of his head.

Slowly Michael pulled back. "I bet you're regretting moving here now, huh?"

The expression Cam gave him surprised Michael. There was no frustration or annoyance at being saddled with a defective mate. The look on his mate's face was tender, supportive, and sweet. Michael would love to be able to wake up to that same expression every day for the rest of his life.

"There is nothing you could have told me that would make me regret meeting you. You're mine, Michael, the sooner you realize that, the better off we'll both be," Cam said, a note of authority in his voice.

He swallowed the lump in his throat and blinked back his tears. He nodded slowly, not sure what else to do.

"I'm sorry your father was an ass, and it's probably for the best that he's no longer in town. I'm not sure I could be held accountable for my actions if I were to ever meet the man."

Michael watched in fascination as Cam's jaw clenched. He could see the hardening of his muscles even through the beard. "Patricia and George Packard have been really good to me. They took me in when Patricia banished my father."

"They sound like wonderful people, and I look forward to getting to know them better in time."

Michael took note of the phrasing and hoped that meant his mate planned to stick around.

"They are," he said and then paused hesitantly before taking a deep breath and plunging head on. "I know they're looking forward to getting to know you better, too."

Cam smiled broadly, then leaned down and gently kissed him. "I know for a fact my parents will go nuts about you just as soon as I tell them."

Michael's heart sank a little at that. Why hadn't Cam told his folks that he'd met his mate? Could he truly be disappointed in who his mate was?

"The only reason I haven't mentioned anything to them yet is I know as soon as I mention that I've met my mate, they will be on the next flight down. I want to keep you to myself for just a little bit longer before my crazy family descends and starts filling your head will all sorts of lies about me."

Michael chuckled, relieved and overwhelmed all at the same time, asking skeptically, "Are you sure they would be lies?"

Cam nodded. "Hell yeah. Anything any member of my family tells you about me is a lie. Don't believe a single word."

Michael chuckled. He thought he might like to meet these people. Cam certainly loved them very much.

He wondered what it would be like to be a part of a loving family again. His mother had died when he'd been too young to know what was going on. He couldn't understand at the time where his mom had gone and why she was no longer there. His dad had tried, but once the drinking started, everything turned to shit.

Patricia and George were wonderful people. They'd opened their home and family to Michael when he had no one and nowhere else to go. However, he'd always felt like he was intruding, like he didn't really belong. Now for what could possibly the first time in his recollection, he might actually have someone to call his own.

A place to call home, and maybe even a family.

"I'll keep that in mind when I meet them," he placated his mate. Michael wanted to hear every single story Cam's family had to tell about the big, scruffy fireman.

"Whatever you need, I'm more than happy to help you with, I hope you realize that." Cam paused as he stared at Michael, his gaze unwavering in the flickering firelight. Eventually Michael nodded. "If you want to take classes to get your GED, I'll do what I can to help. We have a couple of spare rooms. We could set one up as a study."

"*We* have?" he asked in confusion.

Cam sighed a little. "Michael, you are my mate, and this is my house. I hope you'll move in here with me when you're ready and we can start our life together. We're mates. I know it will happen. I'm willing to be patient until you're ready. But the second you agree, what's mine becomes yours and vice versa."

Crap. The man was willing to give him half his house that he'd worked hard for most his life? How the hell was Michael supposed to match that? The most expensive thing Michael had his name attached to was his phone, and the only reason he had that was because Patricia had given it to him. It wasn't one of the latest, greatest models that had everything but the kitchen sink, but it did the job Michael wanted it to and he cherished it.

"You can't do that, Cam," he said as he shook his head and tried to pull away. Cam kept his hold on him, not letting Michael go anywhere.

"Yes, I can. It's my house and I can do what I want with it."

"I can't...I can't pay you for it... I don't have anything to give you." Michael ducked his head in shame, the reality of his situation hitting him all the harder in that moment.

Cam moved a finger under his chin and lifted his face until they were once again looking at one another. "I didn't ask you for anything, I know if our situations were reversed, you would be doing the same thing I am."

Michael didn't even need to think about that one. He would do anything to make his mate happy. Cam must have seen his answer in Michael's expression.

"Now, I'm more than happy to teach you how to drive if you would like. I have a couple of days off. We could go out to the running lands and practice in the parking lot out there if you wanted."

Michael's heart picked up. "Really?"

He couldn't believe Cam would take the time to teach him to drive. The thought of getting behind the wheel of a car after so long dreaming about it had him practically bouncing where he sat.

"Yes." Cam chuckled. "As for right now, how about we head back to the kitchen and you can help me with dinner?"

Just then, Michael heard the undeniable sound of a stomach rumbling. He knew it hadn't been his own, which meant Cam was hungry. Michael immediately felt guilty for pulling the man away from his preparation earlier. If it wasn't for him, they would more than likely have been eating by now.

"Sorry," he said quietly.

"Nothing to be sorry about. Come on." Cam quickly kissed Michael again and then stood. He banked the fire and switched off the tree lights, then took one of Michael's hands and led him back the way they had come to the kitchen.

. . .

MICHAEL COULDN'T BELIEVE HOW MUCH FUN HE WAS having cooking with Cam. His mate took things slow, explaining what he was doing and had Michael helping him every step of the way. Even though Cam had started on the vegetables before they'd been sidetracked with their talk, he hadn't gotten all that far as he'd been too busy talking with Michael.

The salmon had defrosted nicely, and once the vegetables were on, Cam took him through the lemon cream sauce he was going to make to complement the fish.

Twenty minutes after they walked back into the kitchen, they were seated at Cam's small table with their late dinner and a couple of cold beers.

Michael moaned in delight when he tried his first bite of the grilled salmon with the sauce. The fish was juicy and flaky and perfectly cooked, the sauce thick, rich and creamy, the lemon subtle, not overpowering. Michael quickly swallowed and dove in for another bite. He glanced across the table and noticed Cam not eating. The man was just sitting there holding his utensils aloft, staring at Michael.

"Is something wrong with dinner? Did I do something to ruin it? I thought it tasted amazing," Michael quickly said, too nervous he might have ruined something somehow and not realized.

Cam shook his head. "I'm sure the food is perfect."

"Then what's the problem?" Michael asked worriedly.

"I was just trying to reason with my bear that it wouldn't be prudent to leap across the table, tackle you to the ground, and have my wicked way with you." Cam shrugged, as if that statement was no big deal.

Michael swallowed, his bear stirring within. He thought it sounded like an absolutely brilliant plan.

"Um…" Michael really didn't know what to say to that, even if his bear wanted to nod and give his approval to the plan.

Cam grinned roguishly at him, and Michael had to swallow the sudden lump in his throat. "If you could kindly refrain from making those noises, I might—emphasis on the *might*—be able to make it through dinner without molesting you."

Cam then took a bite of his food, his eyes never leaving Michael.

He couldn't hold his mate's intense gaze for long and eventually looked down. He took a long drink of his beer and then started eating again. His mate let him have the silence for a couple of minutes and then started asking more questions. Nothing strenuous or stressful, just light, easy questions. They sat there together, ate their meal, and got to know one another. By the time Cam stood to gather their plates and take them back into the kitchen, Michael had learned quite a bit about his mate.

Michael followed Cam into the kitchen and then picked up a dishtowel as Cam ran hot water in the sink for the dishes. "I was just going to leave these for tomorrow."

"Nah, it's easier to get them done now so they're out of the way and we can forget about them."

Cam nodded his agreement and started washing.

"So, what's your all-time favorite movie?" Michael asked, continuing their earlier talk.

"Would have to say *Shawshank Redemption*. Tim Robbins and Morgan Freeman were awesome in that film."

Michael nodded. He'd seen the movie and thoroughly enjoyed it himself.

They went back and forth asking and answering more questions as they quickly made their way through the dishes. Cam helped Michael by pointing out where all the items belonged once they were clean and dry.

"Favorite song?" he asked as Cam picked up the last pot to wash.

His mate didn't even have to think about that. "Anything by Bon Jovi. Love his music. I've been listening to him since I was a kid. It doesn't hurt that even now the man is still sexy as fuck."

Cam waggled his brows at Michael and grinned impishly. That particular expression was not meant to be seen on a six foot three, two hundred thirty pound, muscled grizzly shifter with facial hair. Michael couldn't help it. He burst out laughing.

His mate watched him for a second before he flicked him with water. Michael tried to defend himself with the towel, but the thing was already damp from all the dishes and really wasn't that large. Cam had an entire sink at his disposal.

Michael couldn't help but laugh and giggle as he

tried to dance out of Cam's way as the man continued to splash water at him.

"You wanna laugh at me, eh?"

Michael nodded, still not able to get himself under control. The look on his mate's face was etched in his mind and every time he thought about it, he broke into more peals of laughter.

Cam chased him around the butcher's block, mirth evident on the bigger man's face. Michael's shirt was now wet and sticking to his skin. Cam reached out and caught hold of him. Just as his mate grabbed him and pulled Michael close, Cam stepped on a wet patch on the tile and his foot went out from under him. Cam went down, holding Michael close as he took the brunt of the impact with the ground.

Cam grunted when he hit, but soon forgot any momentary pain he might have felt when Michael scrambled to sit up on top of him.

He groaned when Michael's ass came in contact with his groin as the man straddled him. Michael started rubbing across his chest, his mate's expression concerned, no longer filled with laughter and joy. Cam didn't like the change at all.

"Are you all right? Did you hurt yourself?" his mate asked frantically as his hands continued to roam.

"I'm fine," Cam reassured him.

"But you groaned. That means something hurts," Michael tried to reason.

His mate was moving on top of him, probably not

even conscious of the fact that he was the one causing Cam's groans.

He reached out and gripped Michael's hips firmly, holding them in place and stopping the man from rubbing up and down against him.

Michael looked puzzled for a minute before his eyes widened and his cheeks flushed the most amazing shade of pink.

Cam let go of the man's hips, took hold of his shoulders, and rolled his mate beneath him, careful not to cause Michael any pain in the process.

When Cam finally had his mate under him, he framed Michael's face in his larger hands, then leaned down and kissed him.

The kiss started sweetly but soon turned intense and heated. Michael squirmed and wriggled, but instead of pushing Cam away like he expected, Michael pulled him in closer. Cam ground his pelvis down, letting his mate feel exactly what the younger man did to him. Michael copied his movements. He had to wrestle with his bear not to tear Michael's clothes from his body when he felt the bulge in Michael's pants.

Cam pulled back from the kiss reluctantly, knowing where they were couldn't be all that comfortable for his mate and not wanting to pressure Michael into anything the man wasn't ready for. The sight of Michael, lips swollen and glistening, his eyes heavy lidded had him taking a firm hold on his animal. Cam had never had so much trouble controlling his other side before.

They were taught as kids about finding their

mates and about how intense the attraction and desire to complete the bond could be. Even with growing up learning about it, Cam had had no idea. He had no point of reference he could compare this with. Until it actually happened, these feelings couldn't be comprehended.

The sensation of fingers threading through his short hair snapped him out of his thoughts, and Cam once again focused on Michael.

"Hey," he said stupidly.

His mate beamed at him. "Hey."

He chuckled and leaned down to kiss the tip of Michael's nose. He stared at the man beneath him, the shy smile shining back at him, and he took the plunge.

"Would you like to move this to a more comfortable location?"

Michael's grin brightened, even if his eyes were a little hesitant. "Where did you have in mind?"

"My bedroom, although if you're not comfortable with that, it's okay. We can always head back to the living room and the fire there," he reassured, wanting Michael to be at ease.

His mate seemed to think it over for a moment and then leaned up and kissed him. "Your bedroom sounds perfect."

Cam stood immediately and held a hand down to help Michael off the floor, not letting go even after his mate was up. Cam led them through the house and down the small hallway to his bedroom. He was constantly touching, petting, pinching, licking and sucking. Michael stumbled a couple of times, but Cam was there to hold him up.

He pulled his smaller mate in against him as they entered his room until Michael was tucked against his chest. Cam bent and placed soft tender kisses to his mate's neck, slowly working his way up the side and along his jaw. Cam burrowed his hands under Michael's clothes until they reached soft warm skin.

Michael tilted his head to the side, giving Cam greater access, the skin on his throat stretched tight. He licked and lightly bit down on the place where he desperately wanted to sink his teeth. His mate arched back against him, the sweetest noises spilling from his mouth. Cam's dick ached in the confines of his pants.

He worked the button on Michael's pants free and slowly lowered the zipper, delving inside the briefs as soon as possible. His mate cried out and thrust up the second Cam's hand came in contact with the steel hardness of his prick. He curled his fingers around Michael's length and slowly started to jack his mate as his lips clamped down on his mate's neck and he started sucking. He wanted his marks on this man so any who saw Michael would know he'd been claimed.

"Oh god, so good," his mate babbled as he pressed back into Cam's solid strength.

The groan that erupted from Michael when Cam reached up with his free hand and twisted one of his nipples was worthy of any porn star. The cock in his hand thickened then released volley after volley of cum as Michael was thrown headfirst into his first orgasm of the night. Cam stroked him a couple more times and then stopped his movements. He knew how sensitive his dick could be after a good release and didn't want to cause his mate any distress.

Michael collapsed against him. Cam released the now dark spot he had been worrying at and, seeing the blissed expression on Michael's face, decided to take matters into his own hands. Cam swung his mate up into his arms.

When he'd suggested they move to the bedroom, Cam had been thinking about his nice soft king-sized mahogany sleigh bed. He hadn't expected to molest his mate when they were barely inside the door, though he really should have figured on it happening.

Cam deposited his happily sated mate on top of the covers. Then he proceeded to strip him of his shoes, clothes, and anything else Cam thought might get in the way of what he had planned, kissing every inch of naked skin as he revealed it. By the time he was finished, Michael had regained his wits and was staring at him with a hunger burning in his eyes.

"You have far too many clothes on," his mate said and then immediately blushed.

Going by what he knew about Michael and his reactions, Cam guessed his mate wasn't very experienced. He wasn't going to embarrass him by calling him out on it, though. Cam would just take things slow.

Cam sat on the edge of his bed and removed his boots and socks, not caring where anything landed, too eager to get back to his waiting mate. He turned back to Michael. His mate was watching his every movement with rapt attention. Cam groaned as he watched Michael's pink tongue slide across the man's lips. Cam lifted the long-sleeve shirt he wore and pulled it off over his head and dropped it to the floor, hoping his mate approved of how he looked.

The sharp inhale from his mate had Cam feeling like a million bucks. He knew he was physically fit, but he'd never thought too much of his body. He'd always believed he was too big, and definitely too hairy.

Unfortunately, being a grizzly bear, it came with the territory.

He'd been told by several men that he should consider waxing it all off. Cam had told them to go shove it. If they didn't like the way he was, he wasn't about to change for them. Michael, on the other hand, he just might consider it for, if he was asked, although he hoped not. The golden brown hair covered his chest and abdomen and went all the way down until it joined in with the hair surrounding his cock.

Michael lay on the bed, his eyes trained on Cam's every movement. His mate bit his lower lip. Cam held back the groan that wanted to escape at the sight.

His mate's eyes remained fastened on him when he reached down and flicked open the button on his jeans, then lowered the zipper. Cam pushed his pants down, exposing his thick thighs, also covered in golden brown hair. He glanced up when he heard a moan and stepped out of his pants, leaving him in nothing but his black boxer briefs, with his hard dick clearly defined behind the skintight material.

"Like what you see?" he asked his mate, the man's eyes still riveted on Cam's package. He didn't get an answer. "Michael?"

His mate shook his head and looked up, meeting Cam's gaze. "Huh?"

Cam laughed. He couldn't help it. He'd never had this kind of effect on someone before, and he was finding that he liked it immensely. Believing Michael had been alone on the bed for too long, he quickly shucked his underwear and then crawled onto the bed until he was hovering over his mate.

Michael watched him the entire way, then wrapped his arms around Cam's neck when he stopped moving.

"Hey," his mate said quietly.

"Hey there, beautiful."

Cam lowered his body and kissed his mate. The second their naked flesh touched, Cam thought his skin was on fire. Tingles and sparks raced through him, all seeming to culminate in his dick, which was harder than he could ever remember. His mate's almost satiny smooth skin contrasted his own hairy one, but Cam loved the differences between them. Michael felt incredible against him.

Michael roamed his hands down Cam's back, digging his fingers in and grabbing a tight hold every time Cam gently thrust against the man. The sweet little noises Michael made were swallowed in their kisses. He wrapped one arm underneath Michael's hips and pulled him close, his mate cried out again as their pricks came in contact, sliding deliciously against one another.

Cam lost all trace of time as they lay there making out. Eventually, he pulled away from the kiss. The little whine he heard had him grinning.

"I'm not going very far," he reassured his mate.

Michael nodded and Cam started kissing his way down the silky body below him. The dark pink nipples stood puckered and erect, taunting Cam to taste them. He licked at the tight skin, trailing his tongue around the area before he lightly nipped at the tip and took it into his mouth, sucking and licking. Michael arched beneath him, grabbing hold of Cam's head and pressing him down. While Cam bit and licked at one nipple, he pinched and rolled the other one, then swapped places.

By the time he was ready to move on, Michael was panting heavily, his hips thrusting up against the air. He had one hand buried in Cam's hair, holding on for dear life, and the other clutched the blankets under him.

"Cam." The sound of his name said like that, almost pleading, begging, made his bear roar with happiness.

He pulled off the slightly swollen little nub and kissed his way down farther until he got to the main prize. Michael's prick was the perfect size, not overly large or thick. It stood tall and aching, the head an angry red color. There was a small bead of precum that had dripped from it. Cam bent and licked up the precious liquid.

The flavor of his mate burst across his palate, salt and sweet all at once. Cam licked until he was sure he'd got it all, then glanced up at Michael. The man's eyes were half closed with pleasure, his cheeks and neck a lovely shade of pink, his nipples swollen from

Cam's earlier activities. The man looked well-loved and Cam intended to keep him that way.

"Cam, so close... God, what you do to me," Michael panted.

He licked up the length of Michael's shaft at the same time he gently pushed the tip of his index finger against his mate's opening. Michael cried out, his hips thrust, and then Cam watched in awe as his mate rode out his second orgasm of the night. White ropes of seed painted his stomach and fine trembles made their way through Michael's body as the man came down from his high. He collapsed into the mattress. The tight grip Michael had on the blankets loosened and he let go.

"Cam," his mate whispered.

"Hmmm," he replied as he bent and started cleaning his mate up, the taste of Michael's release even more intense than that of his precum earlier.

When he was finished, he once again crawled up his mate's body and kissed the man. Michael was practically boneless under him. He sat back, straddling his mate as he took in his mate's blissed-out expression.

Michael's shaft twitched under him, and he raised an eyebrow at his young mate. "Ready for more?"

"What did you have in mind?" Michael reached out and wrapped his soft fingers around Cam's dick. Cam cursed at the unexpected move. His mate lay there and slowly stroked him.

"You want to suck me, love?"

Michael nodded, his eyes blazing with heat. Cam hurried to get into position, eager to feel his mate's lips wrapped around his prick. He moved forward until he was holding on to the headboard above Michael and leaned over until his hard cock was where it needed to be.

His grip on the solid wood tightened at the first hesitant touch of Michael's tongue to his prick, letting him explore at his own pace. He wanted his innocent mate to take his time and enjoy the experience.

Little licks soon became longer ones, and then Cam's shaft was surrounded by moist heat as Michael took him into his mouth.

"Not too much, love. Just a little at a time," he coached, not wanting Michael choking himself. "Wrap your hand around the base, yes, just like that, use it as a guide."

Cam bent his head, watching the entire performance. The sight of his cock sliding in and out of his mate's mouth had him close to exploding in record time. He watched for another minute or two, Michael's movements becoming more certain, happy. When the man hummed, Cam had to pull away lest he explode then and there. Michael looked up and him, panting slightly.

"Did I do something wrong?" he asked, uncertainty written on his face.

"You did everything perfectly. If I hadn't pulled away, I would have come."

"Would that have been so bad?"

"Not at all, and maybe next time we can do that, but for now, my bear is riding me hard to mark you as mine, and to do that I need to come inside your ass."

Michael's eyes widened, and then he nodded

rapidly, a happy grin on his face. Cam chuckled and scooted back a little. He leaned over, opened the top drawer of his bedside table, and pulled out his well-used bottle of lube.

Lube in hand, Cam positioned himself back between Michael's legs, and he noticed Michael's prick had once more filled, lying hard and thick against his mate's stomach.

"You might want to turn over on to all fours. It will be easier the first time like that."

Michael scrambled to fulfill Cam's suggestion. He was sitting in the wrong place and ended up with a foot to the side as his mate attempted to roll over. He grunted at the unexpected impact, and Michael's eyes went wide.

"Oh crap! I'm sorry, sorry."

Cam chuckled and smacked the man lightly on an exposed butt cheek. "It's fine. It didn't hurt, more surprised me than anything."

"Sorry." Michael managed to turn on to his hands and knees without further incident.

The sight that greeted Cam made his mouth water: his mate's firm, tight globes, his light pink puckered hole, and just the faintest dusting of hair. Cam couldn't resist. He leaned down and swiped his tongue over his mate's entrance. Michael quivered and moaned.

Cam leaned in and did it again, and again. His mate writhed beneath him, hissing and groaning as Cam probed deeper. Wanting more, he pulled back and flicked open the bottle of lube. His dick ached and was so fucking hard. He drizzled a generous amount of the viscous liquid down Michael's crack, spreading the cool gel with his fingers. His mate's breath stuttered when Cam pressed one finger deep inside him. The man was so fucking tight, Cam didn't know if he would be able to fit inside.

"You okay?" he asked when Michael stilled.

"Yeah…so good," was the breathy reply.

Cam continued to pump his finger, slowly loosening his mate. "Ready for another one?"

His mate bobbed his head.

Cam slowly pressed a second digit inside to join the first. Michael instantly tightened his grip on the bedsheets, and the muscles in his mate's back contracted, his mate tensing all at once. Then Michael breathed out slowly, relaxing. Cam waited, only moving again when his mate was ready.

They built up to three fingers, and by the time Cam believed his mate was ready to take him, Cam thought he might explode with only a mere touch to his prick.

"Please, *mate*, please." Michael moaned as he pressed back against the fingers, now sliding easily inside him. Cam found the spot he wanted and lightly rubbed his fingers against it. Michael cried out. "Fuck, fuck…so close, again."

Cam would indulge his mate another time, right now, though, he needed inside like he needed another breath. He slowly removed his fingers, Michael protesting every inch of the way.

He chuckled. "I'm not going anywhere, love. Now try to relax and remember to breathe."

Michael nodded frantically, not saying anything.

Cam quickly slicked his cock and lined it up. He slowly pressed forward. He gritted his teeth so he didn't lose it in the tight heat of his mate's ass.

Cam's bear wanted to surface. His fingers tingled and claws broke through, his teeth sharpened, his body hair grew that tiny bit longer. Inch by slow inch, Cam sank deeper inside his mate as he wrestled for control of his body with his animal. When he finally bottomed out, he stilled, wanting to allow Michael all the time he needed to get used to the feeling of being filled. He gripped his mate's hips firmly, his sharp claws pressing but not breaking the skin.

Michael breathed deeply, then wiggled and pressed back. That was the only signal Cam needed. He pulled back until just the head of his dick remained clenched within and then thrust forward. His mate cried out and lowered his head and shoulders to the pillows, accentuating his ass.

The sound of their flesh smacking together, the feel of hips beneath his hands, and the heat surrounding his length as he plunged deep time after time inside his mate had Cam's orgasm barreling forward.

"Fuck," he growled, his voice low and deep.

"Cam…fuck…harder." Michael groaned as he met Cam's hips thrust for thrust.

Not one to disappoint, Cam added more power to his strokes.

He reached down and lifted his mate up so they were pressed together. Michael reached out and took hold of the headboard, steadying himself. He cried out since the angle change had Cam's dick sliding over his prostate with his thrusts.

"Gonna. Please." Michael tilted his head to the side and bared his neck.

Cam didn't hesitate. They were mates, made for each other. They might not know everything about the other yet, but that would come with time. He growled low and then leaned down and bit, hard. His teeth sank into the taut flesh and muscle, puncturing deep within. Cam reached down and took Michael's hard length in his hand. The second he touched it, his mate shouted as his orgasm washed over him.

Michael clamped down on Cam's dick like a vise. He thrust twice more and then threw his head back, roaring as he plunged head first into his own orgasm. Cam clutched his mate as they rode out their pleasure. His heart beat a million miles a minute, and his hand pressed against Michael's chest told him his mate's was as well.

"Wow," Michael said softly.

"You can say that again." They fell to the bed, wrapped around one another.

Cam softened as they lay together, and he slowly slipped from inside his mate. Michael hissed quietly, but Cam still heard it.

"Did I hurt you?" he asked, concerned he'd been too rough with his mate.

"I'm fine," Michael said and patted his leg in reassurance.

Cam didn't believe him entirely and slowly got up to go to the bathroom and get a cloth.

There wasn't an en suite, but with it just being

him, Cam'd had no need of one. The main bath was just through the door to his room anyway and was a decent size. He quickly cleaned himself up and then went back into his room to tend to his mate.

He found Michael passed out on the covers.

One of the selling points when he'd purchased this house was just how big the master bedroom was. Cam was a big guy and big guys needed lots of room. In one corner, he had a small two-seater couch with a square coffee table, which held his laptop. He also needed a nice, large bed to spread out in and, now, to share with his mate.

He also had a decent walk-in closet, which Cam had only managed to fill half of. He hoped in time Michael might like to fill the other half.

As he stood there and took in the sight before him, he remembered everything his young mate had told him earlier. He could only guess at what little Michael had had growing up and hoped his mate would be happy with Cam here.

He felt anger once again start to rise as he thought about what Michael's father and, to a lesser extent, his brother had put him through. No one should be treated that way. Thankfully the men were no longer in town. There was no way Cam would be able to control himself if he ever met them.

He shook his head, wanting to get his thoughts back to more pleasant imaginings.

He walked over to his passed-out mate and quickly cleaned him up, then threw the cloth into a corner. Tomorrow he'd deal with it.

Cam gently pulled the covers and blankets out

from beneath Michael and tucked him in. He flicked off the lights and made his way to the other side of the bed, then crawled under the covers himself. Cam pulled Michael against his chest. The sweet scent of his mate filled his senses as he drifted off to sleep, truly happy and content for the first time in his life.

MICHAEL JOLTED AWAKE, CRYING OUT AS HE ONCE again felt the flames licking at his skin. He bolted upright, patting at his arms hoping to put the fire out. Arms wrapped around him from behind, and he screamed, unaware of what was happening, still caught in the fog of his nightmare.

"Shh…Michael, it's okay, you're safe."

Soft soothing words repeated over and over again finally penetrated his brain. He turned and blinked several times as he tried to clear the images in his mind. Cam's face finally came into focus, and Michael sobbed as he launched himself at his mate.

The man probably thought he was the world's biggest wuss, but he couldn't help it. He'd never had dreams like this before, and Michael just didn't know how to cope with them.

His mate scooted back so he was leaning against the headboard and positioned Michael on top of him. He wrapped Michael up in his strong arms and held him close, Michael burrowing his head into the curve of Cam's throat. His mate's large hands rubbed up and down his back as Cam continued to whisper to him.

"Do you want to talk about it?" his mate asked quietly after a time.

Michael shook his head. He wanted to forget about it.

"It might help to get things out in the open," Cam said in that wonderful soothing tone the man had. Michael sighed and held on a little tighter. "I'm a firefighter, babe, if there's one thing I know about, it's fires… Well, fires and cattle, but you aren't having nightmares about raging bulls by any chance, are you?"

Michael pulled back and stared at his mate in astonishment. The wide grin on Cam's face had Michael chuckling lightly as he snuggled back down. "No bulls this time. If I ever do, though, you'll be the first person I tell."

Cam's body shook slightly underneath him. "As it should be."

Michael sighed, still a little shocked that this big, strong man seemed to want him as much as he did. He had a feeling that even if there wasn't a mating bond between them, Cam would still want him, and the thought made little butterflies in his gut take flight. Michael sighed and started talking.

Cam listened and never interrupted him, letting Michael get everything out in the open. Only when he finally lapsed into silence did Cam pick up the reins and start to tell him about all his experiences with fire, some of the close calls he'd had in his years as a firefighter, and all about his training and how to deal with a fire.

Michael listened and gradually relaxed. He wasn't

sure he would ever want to come face to face with another fire, unsure if he would freeze again or not, but hopefully now after their talk and gaining a better understanding of things, the nightmares would lessen.

They had talked for several hours and now the sun was just starting to peek above the horizon. Michael settled down to sleep, once again held close in Cam's arms. For the first time since the fire, he wasn't scared to close his eyes, and he had his wonderful mate to thank for that.

8

———

Christmas morning dawned bright and early, and Michael woke alone for the first time in three days. He didn't like the feeling. He couldn't believe how fast he'd gotten used to sleeping in Cam's arms. The nightmares had all but gone, and Michael had managed to get a full night's sleep on the last night he'd been at his mate's place. Well, as full as it could be when his mate was waking him every couple of hours to ravish him from head to toe, but Michael wasn't about to complain about that.

They'd spent their time getting to know one another better, and Cam gave Michael the promised driving lessons. Michael really believed that Cam meant everything he said and would help him get his life in order to where he wanted it to be. He still had no idea what he wanted to do, but he hoped he would have a better grasp of things once he at least got a chance to finish high school.

Michael hadn't wanted to leave Cam yesterday, but

the man had to go to work. He knew Cam's work was important to him, and as much as he hated being separated from his mate, Michael would deal. Hopefully it would get easier once they'd been together for a while. Right now his skin was crawling and he desperately wanted to see his mate.

Cam had dropped him off yesterday morning back at the Packards' house after they'd stopped at one of the many pancake restaurants and eaten breakfast together. He'd told Michael he was more than happy for him to stay at their house.

Their house—that was what Cam kept calling it.

He loved that his mate was so willing to share everything already even though they'd only known each other a short time. Michael just wished he had something he could share back. He had no illusions that things between them would be smooth sailing from here on out. They would have their arguments and fights as they slowly learned everything about each other and their likes and dislikes. Michael just hoped they didn't find anything they couldn't get past. He really thought he could fall in love with Cam.

He'd thought it would be easier, at least for last night, if he went back to the Packards'. He didn't have a car and it would save them having to take time out on Christmas to come and pick him up. It wasn't until he walked back inside the house and Patricia herded him right back out again that he was thankful for the small amount of time he had to himself.

Michael hadn't even thought about a present for his mate, let alone having enough money to buy the man something nice. Patricia had kindly taken care of that for him.

Because mom's can fix anything. She hadn't even made him feel bad about it.

They'd gone shopping and had a wonderful afternoon even though the stores were packed with last-minute shoppers. Michael was a little nervous about giving Cam his gift. He really hoped his mate liked it. Cam worked until midafternoon, meaning Michael had to wait most of the day before he got to see his mate again.

Reluctantly, Michael got out of bed. The house was cold in the early morning. Through his bedroom window he saw snow coming down outside. He grabbed his towel and made his way to the bathroom.

After a nice hot shower, Michael dressed in an old faded pair of jeans with a long-sleeved shirt and added a pair of socks. His poor toes were a little cold this morning. Michael slowly walked out to the kitchen. The sounds of utensils clanking and quiet talking met him as he walked through the door.

"Morning," he said softly.

"Morning. Merry Christmas," George said as he smiled up at him from where he sat at the kitchen table drinking a cup of coffee.

"Merry Christmas," Michael replied.

"Merry Christmas, honey," Patricia said as she left the little electric fry pan she was using and walked over to give him a hug and kiss on the cheek.

Most of the kitchen was still unusable. After the holidays, contractors would be coming in to rip out the burnt remains and replace them with Patricia's new kitchen. Still terribly guilt-ridden about what had happened, Michael kept apologizing, but neither Patricia nor George were mad at him about it.

"Would you like a cup of coffee?"

"No, thanks. I think I might get some juice this morning."

"Okay, the boys should be over shortly. The first round of pancakes will be ready in a minute. Would you mind getting the syrup and placing it on the table for me?"

The new plan for Christmas was to have breakfast and a very light lunch here, then head over to Christian and Vincent's place. Patricia had spent half the day there yesterday baking and getting things organized before she'd come home and taken Michael out shopping. Christian and his mate were staying home to get ready for their family dinner later that night, but the other Packard boys would be here for breakfast.

By the time Michael poured himself a glass of juice and grabbed the syrup, Patricia was placing a plate on the table with a small stack of pancakes in its center. Michael sat and waited for George to take a couple first before he reached over and served himself some breakfast. Bobby and Julius arrived not long after and they all spent a lovely, stress-free morning together.

BEFORE MICHAEL REALIZED IT, THE MORNING HAD flown by and they were all piling into the cars to make their way over to Christian's place. Michael was clutching the wrapped present for Cam to his chest.

He glanced at his watch for what felt like the millionth time that day and moaned. He still had several more hours before his mate would get off work.

They arrived several minutes later, and after a few trips to unload the car of presents and food, they were ensconced inside the nice warm house. Christian had a fire going in the fireplace, the television was playing some old Christmas movie—that Michael had seen a million times before—and the Christmas tree was strung with garlands of tinsel and strings of what looked to be old lights. The aromatic fragrance of pine filled the room. The only thing missing from the scene was Christmas music, and then it would be perfect.

Michael was still a little overwhelmed at how the Packards' had opened their arms to him and, now that he'd found his mate, had happily included Cam in their plans as well.

The opening of presents had been held back to make sure everyone was there to enjoy it together. Michael was a little upset that he hadn't been able to get anything for Patricia and George, especially after everything they had done for him. He swore that, as soon as he could, he would buy them something showing them the depth of his gratitude and how much he had grown to love them.

Michael wandered into the kitchen to see both Patricia and Vincent hard at work. Patricia had gone straight to the kitchen and taken over preparations for their Christmas dinner.

"Can I help with anything?" he asked, knowing he

couldn't do much but willing to help out any way he could.

"No, honey, why don't you go join the others and relax for a while. Vincent and I have things well in hand." Patricia smiled before she turned back to her pot.

"Okay, call out if you need me to help."

"We will," she assured him.

On the way back to the living room, Michael passed the dining area, thinking maybe he could help by setting the table. Vincent, however, had been a very busy man. The large table was covered with a stunning deep red tablecloth and was laden with plates, utensils, glasses, and cloth napkins in silver rings. A large glass piece sat in the center of the table with a thick red candle housed within, and it was nestled in a wreath of green pine needles and brown pinecones. The table looked simple yet elegant at the same time and left plenty of room for the plates of food to be placed in the center.

On the sideboard to the left of the room sat dessert, already made and ready to go—pecan pie, chocolate Yule log, and a cherry pie. Michael's mouth watered as he gazed at them, and he wondered if they would consider starting with dessert. Even though the smells coming out of the kitchen were amazing, dessert looked incredible and was ready now.

Michael decided he better get out of there before he did something stupid like taste test the goods, and headed to the living room where George and his three sons were lounging around watching a movie. Everyone told him to sit and join them so Michael did, even if he wasn't at all interested in seeing *Miracle on 34th Street* again.

The afternoon passed quickly, drinks were handed out occasionally, there was much yelling at the television and some good-natured banter between brothers, even some between father and sons. Michael watched in fascination, he'd never spent a more relaxing, enjoyable time with family before. When his father and brother had still been there, there was more drinking and lots more yelling. However, none of it was in good spirits. Most of the time, Michael had tried to confine himself to his room, hoping his father would forget about him entirely.

The doorbell rang, surprising Michael out of his thoughts. He leapt up.

"I'll get it if that's all right?" he asked Christian. Michael didn't want to step on his Alpha's toes by assuming he could answer the door.

Christian chuckled. "Go right ahead, Michael. It's more than likely for you anyway."

Michael grinned, hoping the man was right, then practically raced to the front door. He could hear the quiet snickers behind him, but he didn't care.

He opened the door and let out an unmanly squeal when he was lifted off his feet and pulled hard up against Cam's body. He felt something hit against his back as Cam ducked his head and kissed him for all he was worth. Michael forgot about everything, where he was, who was there, what had hit him; all he knew in that moment was that he was once again in the arms of his mate and everything in the world felt right.

Another minute would have seen Michael throw his arms around Cam's neck and wrap his legs around the man's middle. The clearing of a throat behind him, however, stopped Michael before he could get too carried away.

"Cameron," Patricia said with genuine warmth in her tone. "Glad you could make it."

"Patricia, thank you for including me in your holiday celebrations." Cam pulled Michael in close to his side and held him there. Michael looked down and saw his mate was carrying a large brown paper carry bag with several wrapped gifts inside.

"Of course, you're welcome. Come in, come in. You have perfect timing. Dinner should be ready in roughly half an hour. Enough time that we can open the presents before we sit down to eat." Patricia's eyes lit at the mere mention of presents.

The ex-Alpha was one giant kid at heart it would seem.

Vincent wandered in from the kitchen and everyone took a seat in the living room. The television was turned off, and Julius had the honor of being Santa, handing out all the gifts. Before Cam sat down, he handed over the bag with the gifts to add to the ones already under the tree.

Names were called, presents were handed out, and soon the room was filled with the sounds of paper ripping and people exclaiming over their gifts. Michael held his breath as his mate looked shocked when he was handed the present Michael had gotten for him. He kissed Michael and then opened it.

Michael finally let out his pent-up breath at the look of excitement and happiness that crossed Cam's features as he unwrapped the black leather jacket Patricia had helped Michael buy for his mate.

"If you don't like it or it doesn't fit, we can take it back and get you something else," he said nervously. He thought his mate liked it, but he could never be too sure.

"I love it!" Cam exclaimed as he stood and pulled on the jacket. It fit perfectly, and Michael blushed a little as he remembered trying to convey to the salesclerk how large Cam was. "Thank you, love."

Cam sat again and kissed him. Even though the kiss was short, Michael felt the coiled heat in it.

Confusion filled Michael when Julius handed him a gift. Michael really hadn't expected to be getting anything today. He'd already resigned himself to that fact. He stared down at the little tag, his mate's name scrawled in flowing letters across the bottom of it.

"When on earth did you have time to get me anything?" he asked.

"I have my ways. Now open it." Cam grinned at him.

Michael wanted to melt under the man's gaze. He ripped the wrapping and sat there, stunned, as he stared down at the box to a brand-new iPad.

"Thank you," Michael choked out, his throat clogged with the tears he was holding back. He'd never in his life had something so precious all for his own.

"You're welcome, love. I figure when you're ready we can sit down and load it with a number of educational applications to help you achieve your goals." Cam looked a little uncertain.

Michael couldn't have that. He couldn't believe how thoughtful his mate had been. "Thank you. I love it."

He leaned in and kissed his mate gently before cuddling in close, his head resting on Cam's large shoulder. His mate wrapped his arms around Michael and held him tight.

Michael was further surprised when he was handed more gifts. Every one of the Packards had gotten him something. Whether it was some new clothes, books, or a gift certificate, Michael didn't care. He thanked them all the same, overwhelmed at their generosity.

"Oh, Michael, Cameron, it's beautiful, thank you," Patricia said as she stared at the gift in her hands.

He pulled away from his mate slightly and looked at the man inquiringly. He hadn't had the means to get the Packards a Christmas gift, so why was Patricia thanking them?

Cam leaned down and whispered in his ear so softly Michael knew no one else would be able to hear him. "I took the liberty for the both of us. I hope you don't mind."

Michael couldn't believe how lucky he felt. Cam was perfect for him and surprised him day after day. There truly was nothing he could have done that would have endeared himself to Michael more. He mouthed the words "Thank you." His mate smiled at him and gave him a small nod.

"We're glad you like it," Cam said gently.

Michael looked over and could see the wood and crystal figurine of a mamma bear with cubs following along behind her.

"Ohh… Thank you, boys, this should go nicely after dinner," George said appreciatively. Michael looked at the older man who had been more a father to him in the last couple of months than his own dad had been in twenty-two years. George was holding up a bottle of dark amber liquid, already licking his lips in anticipation of trying the scotch.

Cam chuckled. "Now don't drink it all at once. I've been told it's a very good bottle."

"No chance of that happening. I'll be savoring it, that's for sure."

Michael watched as Christian asked to have a look and George refused to hand it over, holding the bottle close to his chest like a two-year-old not wanting to give up his favorite toy. The sight made him laugh. Michael was so damn happy.

CAM LOOKED AROUND THE DINING ROOM TABLE, thankful that his mate had found such wonderful people to be in his life after everything he'd been through. He'd taken the plunge that morning and called his parents to wish them a Merry Christmas and inform them he'd met his mate. As he'd predicted, they were planning a trip down just as soon as all the relatives currently visiting for the holidays left.

Christian sat opposite him wearing a purple paper Christmas hat. They'd been handed out when everyone had been seated, Cam himself was wearing a very fetching yellow hat. Utensils clanked as people dished up their plates, and bowls heaped with vegetables were passed, as were platters with carved turkey and ham, candied yams and a big bowl of gravy. Cam stared down at his plate, practically overflowing with food. His stomach growled. He hadn't eaten since lunch at the station in anticipation of this dinner.

They all sat quietly for a moment while George said grace. Once he finished, the only noises around the table were the clatter of utensils as everyone attacked their food. The fact that everyone seated at the table, bar Vincent, was a bear shifter meant there was a great deal of food.

Cam groaned as the rich taste of the gravy-soaked turkey hit his palate. God he loved this time of year. He honestly thought he'd be missing out this year since he'd left his family behind in Montana, but being here with the Packards came in a close second. Cam had no doubt this was Michael's family, and he envisioned a lot more family dinners like this in his future.

After the first couple of minutes, when everyone was too busy stuffing their faces, chatter opened up around the table. They talked, joked, ate, and drank. Cam had finally relaxed completely after his work shift and enjoyed seeing this happy, carefree side of his mate when he paused and sniffed the air.

He pushed his chair back, wanting to put a little distance between him and the overwhelming scents from the table. Cam sniffed again. Something was burning, he was sure of it. After several years being a firefighter, he knew just what he was smelling.

"Do you have an extinguisher?" he asked Christian hurriedly as everyone stared at him in confusion.

"Of course, why?" Christian looked perplexed for a moment until he too raised his head and scented the air. Cam could see the exact moment Christian caught up with him.

"What's going on?" Michael asked.

"I can smell a fire," he said calmly. He glanced at his mate and noticed the way Michael had stiffened. "It's okay, love. Come here, you'll see."

He held his hand out to Michael who nodded and quickly stood, then rushed over to him. Cam couldn't believe how strong his mate was being. Cam's heart had almost broken the other night as Michael poured out all his fears and insecurities and relayed the nightmares to him in graphic detail. Michael's hand slipped into his own much larger one seconds later and they turned to follow Christian.

Christian raced to the cupboard, and Cam met the man to take the extinguisher from him. He followed his nose to the living room, where he was met with the sight of the Christmas tree ablaze in the corner. Michael once again stopped and stiffened.

"It's okay," Cam said reassuringly.

Cam needed to get this put out and now. There

was still paper strewn across the floor from all the presents, the gifts themselves were scattered as well, supplying plenty of fuel for the fire. Just as they stepped forward, Cam pulled the pin on the extinguisher and the fire alarms started blaring.

He could hear the many people behind him talking, but Cam concentrated on what he was doing.

Christmas trees burned fast; he was lucky he'd been here and smelled it early. The entire front half of the house could have gone up in a matter of minutes. The flames hadn't yet managed to spread to the walls, but were starting to lick at the ceiling. Cam maneuvered Michael in front of him and quickly had him take hold of the extinguisher. Together they opened up the spray and doused the flames.

It took some time and he was sure to use the entire contents of the bottle.

All that was left when they were finished was a smoking ruin of a tree. The walls behind and above were lightly scorched, but considering what had happened, it could have been a lot worse. Cam kissed the side of Michael's neck.

"So fucking proud of you, love," he said quietly before he placed the extinguisher on the floor and stepped around his mate, carefully walking forward.

He crouched down to get a better look at the remains of the tree. There was still a fair amount of heat coming off the blackened pile and from what he could see it looked like faulty wiring in the lights could be the culprit. However, he wasn't an investigator and would leave that to the professionals, whom he was sure someone would have called.

Cam checked once more for any hot spots that he thought might flare back to life, but he was happy the fire seemed to be out for good.

"Jesus, man, thank you," Christian said as he walked up and clapped Cam on the shoulder. "That would have been a hell of a lot worse if you hadn't been here. How in the world did you smell that?"

"I have a very keen sense of smell when it comes to fire," Cam said. Michael raced the couple of steps up to him and wrapped his arms around Cam as he stood. His mate was trembling. "Everything's okay. You did brilliantly. Just some faulty wiring, I think."

Michael nodded and held him close. The alarm stopped blaring, and Cam assumed someone had managed to turn the damn thing off. As much as he hated listening to that god-awful sound, the alarms provided a crucial service and saved lives.

"Thank you, son. That's twice now you've come to our rescue," George said as he nodded his appreciation of Cam's fast action.

"It's my job. Anytime I can help."

"The firemen are on their way. I told them Cam was here and the fire was out, but they should be here shortly to check things over," Bobby said as he walked into the slightly smoky living room with a phone still tucked to his ear.

"Thanks. How about we open up some windows and let this smoke dissipate?" he suggested. The cold immediately zapped any warmth from the room, leaving Michael shivering in his arms.

"So, who wants some pie?" Patricia asked, trying to lighten the mood.

His mate stirred in his arms. Patricia's question had certainly gotten someone's attention. Cam laughed.

"Would love some," he announced when he'd gotten his chuckles under control. Cam had seen the desserts resting and waiting on the sideboard and couldn't wait to get a piece of each of them.

He made his way out of the living room, Michael still held against his side. As he walked into the dining room once again, Patricia turned to him.

"I can't tell you how happy I am to have a fireman in the family."

Michael tensed against him slightly before his mate sprang from his arms and darted across the room and launched himself at Patricia. They embraced long and hard.

"Welcome, and thanks," George said again.

"My pleasure," he reassured.

Cam stood there and watched his young mate. Everything wouldn't be smooth sailing from here on out, but no matter what, Cam wasn't going to give up. This man was his life and he was quickly falling in love with him.

As he stood there surrounded by this family that a week ago he'd never met, Cam couldn't think of a better way to spend Christmas, fire and all.

THANK YOU, READERS!

Thank you for purchasing **Wreath of Fire**. We hope you enjoyed this world Toni has created. She loves being able to have more sexy men around to protect people and fight for their love. Who can blame her? Look out for her next book in The Hounds of the Hunt, **Jordan's Accidental Adoption,** coming soon.

Want more *Bears*? Toni will be continuing the *Smokey Mountain Bear* books this winter. Keep an eye out for announcements from Mischief Corner Books.

Want to let us know what you think? Please consider leaving a review where you purchased this ebook or on Goodreads. Reviews and word-of-mouth recommendations are *vital* to independent publishers.

Sincerely,
Mischief Corner Books

ABOUT TONI GRIFFIN

Toni Griffin lives in Darwin, the smallest of Australia's capital cities. Born and raised in the state she's a Territorian through and through. Growing up Toni hated English with a passion (as her editors can probably attest to) and found her strength lies with numbers.

Now, though, she loves escaping to the worlds she creates and hopes to continue to do so for many years to come. She's a single mother of one and works full time. When she's not writing you can just about guarantee that she will be reading one of the many MM authors she loves.

Feel free to drop her a line at info@tonigriffin.net anytime.

Webpage:
http://www.tonigriffin.net

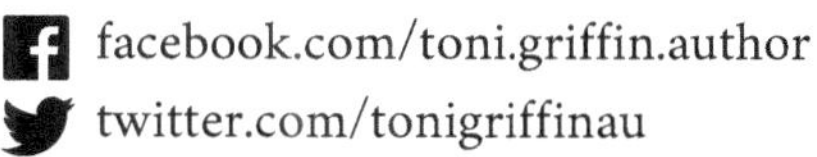

facebook.com/toni.griffin.author
twitter.com/tonigriffinau

SMOKEY MOUNTAIN BEARS
A Bear in the Woods
Wreath of Fire
A Bear's Bear

THE BORILLIAN TWIST
Finding Connor

THE HOLLAND BROTHERS
Unexpected Mate
Determined Mate
Protective Mate
Forbidden Mate
*A Very Holland Christmas**
*A Very Holland Valentine**
A Wolf in Cop's Clothing

*Available together as *A Very Holland Collection*

ABOUT MISCHIEF CORNER BOOKS

Mischief Corner Books is an organization of superheroes... no, it's a platinum-album techno-fusion group... no, hold on a sec here...

Ah yes. Mischief Corner is a small press publisher offering queer romance and fiction for readers, intent on making some mayhem with our books. Diversity and positive representation for all members of the queer community is important to us, and MCB works to make those voices heard because those who travel the off the beaten path are a gift and their stories make the world a more interesting place.

In addition to making mayhem, we live to break molds. MCB. Giving voice to LGBTQ fiction.

Website:
http://www.mischiefcornerbooks.com

facebook.com/MischiefCorner
twitter.com/MischiefCorner

www.ingramcontent.com/pod-product-compliance
Lightning Source LLC
Chambersburg PA
CBHW050346160726
48002CB00001B/484